The Water Closed Over
the Top of Her Head.

I'm drowning.

The thought gave her a fresh spurt of energy. She kicked furiously, ignoring the cramp in her stomach, pushing aside the pain in her chest.

Her head burst up above the surface and Willow gulped frantically, trying to get air without water but unable to control what entered her nose and mouth. She screamed, or at least she thought she screamed, before she went under again.

And that's when it happened. She was still struggling, still aware that she was drowning, when, in her mind, she saw a girl on a small raft made of woven branches. She wore a simple, long white gown, belted at the waist, and her straight black hair hung to her shoulders. She was twelve and her name was Kalos. This black-haired girl looked nothing like Willow, and yet Willow knew immediately that she and Kalos were the same person. She was watching herself, in a different time . . .

Books by Peg Kehret

Nightmare Mountain
Sisters, Long Ago

Available from MINSTREL Books

Sisters, Long Ago

PEG KEHRET

A MINSTREL® BOOK

PUBLISHED BY POCKET BOOKS

New York   London   Toronto   Sydney   Tokyo   Singapore

A Minstrel Book published by
POCKET BOOKS, a division of Simon & Schuster Inc.
1230 Avenue of the Americas, New York, NY 10020

Copyright © 1990 by Peg Kehret
Front cover illustration by Catherine Huerta

Published by arrangement with Cobblehill Books

ISBN: 0-671-73433-4

First Minstrel Books printing March 1992

10 9 8 7 6 5 4 3 2

Special thanks to

*Alice Burgess of the Fred Hutchinson
Cancer Research Center, Seattle, WA.*

King County Public Libraries

FOR MY MOTHER

If I have another life,
I hope she's there

1

NUK UA em ennu en Xu ammu Xu.

Willow stirred in her sleep. Beside her, Muttsie stood, turned in a circle, and curled up again.

Nuk ua em ennu en Xu ammu Xu.

The words floated into her consciousness, waking her gently.

Willow blinked in the darkness and reached for the tablet and pencil. Since she first dreamed of Kalos, she had kept paper and pencil next to her bed. If she had such dreams again, she wanted to write them down before she forgot them. She switched on her lamp.

Nuk ua em ennu en Xu ammu Xu.

She stared at what she had written. She had no idea what the words meant yet she sensed that they were important.

Why? What could this mumbo-jumbo sentence mean?

She said the words out loud. "Nuk ua em ennu en Xu ammu Xu." It was clearly a different language but she didn't know which one. Could it be a code? Did it have something to do with Kalos?

A month earlier, Willow would have gone back to sleep and forgotten the words. But not now. Too many things had happened. Strange things. Odd things, like these nonsense words.

It all began on her birthday.

Willow and her best friend, Gretchen, had walked barefoot on the warm sand, past Camelback Rock, to the cove where the old driftwood log provided a natural table.

Gretchen carried their towels, a Frisbie, a bag of sandwiches, sunscreen, and a pink cardboard carton containing a chocolate birthday cake with thirteen candles on it. She refused to let Willow carry anything.

"You aren't lifting your little pinkie today," Gretchen said. "You're going to lie in the sun and pig out on the picnic."

"Sounds good to me," Willow said.

When they reached the log, Gretchen made a big production out of spreading Willow's towel on the sand for her and handing her the bottle of sunscreen. "You use first, honorable aged one," she said, bowing low.

"Aged one! You sound like I'm your grandmother," Willow said, but she took the oil and began smoothing it on her legs.

"Grandma Willow look youthful for her age. Not seem a day over forty."

Willow finished oiling herself and lay back on her towel,

savoring the warm rays of the sun. It was wonderful to have someone wait on her, for a change.

She didn't mind ironing Sarah's blouses for her, or doing the dishes even when it was Sarah's turn. She felt sorry for her sister and wanted to help her, but she did get weary. Even though Sarah was in remission, she remained frail and tired easily. Her leukemia was always there, hovering over Willow's family like a thundercloud about to burst.

Mr. and Mrs. Paige, Willow's parents, worried constantly about Sarah. Sometimes it seemed to Willow that they thought of nothing else. Other families talked about politics or football games or the neighbors. Willow's parents discussed Sarah's lack of appetite or Sarah's blood count or Sarah's latest nose-bleed. Potential disaster lurked around the corner of each new day.

Willow knew it wasn't Sarah's fault that she was sick. Most of the time, Willow didn't mind doing whatever she could to make Sarah's life easier. Still, it was pleasant to have Gretchen fuss over her today; it felt good to be pampered.

Willow stretched out her arms, wanting to catch the sun in every pore. As the heat entered her body, it soothed her frazzled nerves and calmed her troubled thoughts. She relaxed, lulled by the luxury of laziness.

"Hunk alert!" Gretchen whispered, as she poked Willow in the ribs.

Willow opened her eyes. Squinting in the brightness, she looked at the couple who were spreading towels a short distance down the beach. Gretchen was right. The guy was definitely good looking.

The girl with him jammed a red beach umbrella into the sand, tilting it to get the right angle. Willow watched her lazily, noting the girl's long, single blonde braid and her bright blue swimsuit.

The girl adjusted the umbrella, stepped back, and turned to face Willow. When their eyes met, the girl stopped and stood perfectly still, staring. Her look was so intense that for a moment, Willow thought perhaps the girl was someone she knew.

No. If Willow had seen that long blonde braid before, she would remember it. Probably the girl was looking at her because she realized that Willow had been watching *her*. Embarrassed to be caught staring at a stranger, Willow lay back on her towel and closed her eyes.

She awoke when Gretchen shook her shoulder. "You're scorching," Gretchen said. "Roll over and toast the other side for awhile."

Willow looked at the pink hue on her legs and arms. She felt hot and sticky; she knew she'd be geranium red by evening.

"I need to cool down," she said. "I'm going for a swim."

"Wait for me!"

Together, Gretchen and Willow waded into the lake, shrieking and shivering as the cold water covered their ankles. As Willow tried to get up her nerve to go in farther, Gretchen bellyflopped forward and started to swim. The sudden shower of water caught Willow in the face and she spluttered for a moment before she dove in, too.

She swam steadily but without pushing herself. She knew there was no hope of catching Gretchen—not after Gretchen took off first—so she didn't even try to keep up. Instead, she

4

alternated between a breaststroke and a sidestroke, taking it easy, liking the fluid way her body slid through the water.

The cramp caught her by surprise. She was sidestroking when it hit her. She clutched her stomach and tried to tread water but the cramp was so strong that she doubled over with the pain.

She opened her mouth to yell for help. When her lips parted, no sound came out. Instead, lake water rushed in. The water stung her throat, filling her nose and ears, choking her so that she couldn't think clearly. In her panic, she forgot to move her arms or kick her legs. She could think only about air. The more she struggled to inhale, the worse it got.

The water closed over the top of her head.

I'm drowning.

The thought gave her a fresh spurt of energy. She kicked furiously, ignoring the cramp in her stomach, pushing aside the pain in her chest.

Her head burst up above the surface and Willow gulped frantically, trying to get air without water but unable to control what entered her nose and mouth. She screamed, or at least she thought she screamed, before she went under again.

And that's when it happened. She was still struggling, still aware that she was drowning, when, in her mind, she clearly saw herself as a young child. She was about three years old and she had made a gift for her grandmother: a piece of yellow construction paper filled with red crayon squiggles and lines. Her grandmother held the yellow paper in one hand while she hugged Willow tightly. Her grandfather stood beside them, beaming.

She felt their love. It was a tangible thing, surrounding

her, engulfing her. The room was full of love and Willow felt cherished and secure.

The scene lasted only a fraction of a second and then she saw a different scene. A girl stood on a small raft made of woven branches. She wore a simple, long white gown, belted at the waist, and her straight black hair hung to her shoulders. She was twelve and her name was Kalos. This black-haired girl looked nothing like Willow and yet Willow knew immediately that she and Kalos were the same person. She was watching herself, in a different time.

The raft, which was piled high with grain, floated on a wide river where tall reeds grew along the banks. Kalos moved her head back and forth as she pushed her steering pole into the river, watching carefully for sandbanks or crocodiles. She wasn't far now from the east bank of the river. She would be home soon and her tired muscles were glad of it.

A flock of wild geese rose from the reeds ahead, startling her with their honking and flapping. On the shore, she saw two boys with throwing sticks. The boys took aim and flung the sticks with all their might. Kalos stopped poling and watched to see if either of the sticks would hit its target.

In that brief moment, when she failed to concentrate on the river, her raft struck the huge snout of a crocodile. Enraged, the beast brought its jaws down on the raft, tipping it sideways, spilling the grain into the river. Frantically, Kalos jammed her steering pole into the water, trying to steady the raft and move it out of the crocodile's reach. She was too late. The crocodile snapped again and the raft broke, dumping Kalos into the river.

She clung to the pole as she tried to swim through the thick stand of reeds. The water behind her thrashed violently;

6

she knew the enraged crocodile would spot her at any moment.

Kalos jammed her pole into the river bottom and tried to propel herself faster but it was impossible to move quickly. The reeds tore her clothing and cut her arms. Dark water washed into her mouth and, though she struggled with every bit of strength she possessed, her head sank beneath the surface.

Kalos looked upward, her vision blurred by the murky brown water, and saw the thick stand of reeds close over her. She would be gone without a trace. Her parents and Tiy would never know what had happened to her, or where.

She forced the pole upward, trying to move it forward. Her feet kicked frantically. A large shape, as big as herself, loomed in the water ahead of her.

Kalos quit struggling. Better to drown, she thought, than to be eaten alive by the crocodile.

And then, just as Kalos felt herself losing consciousness, the pole, which she still held in her hand, jerked. For a moment, she thought the crocodile had found her but then, even in her semiconscious state, she realized that the pole was being pulled toward shore. She put her other hand on the pole and held tight. She moved faster, oblivious now to the sharp reeds, thinking only that there was still hope.

Her head surfaced and she took a great gulp of air. She felt the sandy bank of the river beneath her sandals and fought to get her footing. She dropped the pole as hands grasped her, tugging, pulling. Kalos stumbled up the bank, coughing and choking, and fell to her knees. She blinked the water from her eyes and looked at her rescuer.

It was Tiy. Wordlessly, Tiy dropped to her knees and the girls embraced, both crying tears of relief.

After a moment, Kalos sat back on her heels.

"Thank you, my sister," she said.

Tiy did not reply but her dark eyes shone with love.

As Willow watched Kalos and Tiy, she knew the same feeling of love that she'd felt when she saw herself as a little child, with her grandparents. It encircled her, and made her feel safe.

This second scene, vivid though it was, lasted no longer than the first one. It flashed through Willow's brain like a video on fast-forward and was gone almost before it began.

While she saw these odd unrelated scenes in her mind, Willow still kicked frantically, fighting to keep her head above the surface of Pinecone Lake. Instead, she sank deeper in the water, and she felt herself losing consciousness.

As the water closed over her head a third time, Willow saw her grandparents again. They stood together, surrounded by a bright light. Their arms stretched toward her, welcoming her.

2

A HAND grasped Willow's hair, yanking her upward. Another hand moved down her neck; the fingers dug into her shoulder and forced her body up until her head burst above the water.

Willow choked, desperately trying to get air. An arm went securely around her and her rescuer swam toward shore. Willow tried to kick but she had no strength left. She went limp, floating smoothly, grateful for an occasional breath of air.

As they reached the shore, Willow was lifted, carried by many hands, and then laid on her stomach while someone pushed on her back, forcing the lake water she'd swallowed out of her body. Willow choked, vomited, choked again.

At last she could breathe normally. She lay quietly for a moment, face down on the beach, relieved to be alive. Someone handed her a towel; gratefully, she wiped her face.

She rolled over and opened her eyes. The girl with the

braid, the girl Willow had watched earlier, looked down at her.

"Are you OK?" the girl asked.

"Yes. Are you the one who saved me?"

The girl nodded.

"Thank you," Willow said.

They looked at each other again and in that instant Willow knew. This was the same girl she'd seen in her mind, when she was drowning. This girl with the blonde braid once had black hair, black bangs. Long ago, she waded chest deep into a river where a crocodile thrashed in the reeds and saved her sister. Instead of a bright blue swimsuit then, she wore a long, white dress, but it was this same girl. The same, yet different, just as the girl who fell off the raft into the reeds was Willow and yet not Willow. Kalos was a different Willow—the same person in a separate body. The girl with the braid was Tiy, also in a separate body.

Willow didn't know how she knew this. She could not have explained it to anyone but she was as certain of these facts as she was that the sun shone down and the waves lapped the shores of Pinecone Lake.

Gretchen knelt beside her, her eyes wide with worry.

"I think I should call an ambulance," Gretchen said.

Other voices chimed in, giving advice, offering to drive the girls home.

"I'll be all right," Willow said. "I just need to rest."

"I can't believe this happened," Gretchen said. "If you're sure you're OK here, I'll go to the phone booth and call your mom."

"I'm OK."

"Stay right there until I come back."

"I won't move," Willow promised.

She didn't want to move. She wanted to lie still and think about what had happened. The memory from her childhood and the odd scene with the raft had each lasted only a fraction of a moment. Yet both were indelibly imprinted in Willow's mind and each, when she recalled them, gave her a warm, secure feeling: the knowledge that she was loved. As little Willow, she was loved by her grandparents. As Kalos, she was loved by her sister, Tiy.

She looked around for the girl with the braid. The girl was gone.

When Gretchen returned, Willow said, "Will you see if you can find the girl who saved me? I want to talk to her."

Gretchen searched without success until Willow's mother arrived. Mrs. Paige insisted that Willow be examined by a doctor.

The doctor pronounced Willow unharmed but said she should go to bed, and stay there until the next morning.

As they rode home, Willow told her mother exactly what had happened. All except the part about the two scenes in her mind. Somehow, she wasn't ready to talk about them. Not yet.

When Willow got into bed, she fell asleep immediately.

It was dusk when she awoke. Pink light from the setting sun filtered through the white curtains on her bedroom windows. Muttsie was curled beside her like a fur doughnut, having crept in after Willow fell asleep.

Willow lay quietly, thinking about the two scenes she had glimpsed so vividly when she was near drowning, and the intense feeling of love they gave her. She could understand the love between herself and her grandparents. She had adored them all her life and when they died two years ago in a tragic car accident, she mourned deeply. But what was the scene with Tiy all about? Why did she have a feeling of kinship toward the girl with the braid?

Before she could sort out her thoughts, Mrs. Paige came into her room.

"How do you feel?" she asked.

"Hungry."

Mrs. Paige smiled. "I'm glad to hear that," she said. "We'll postpone your birthday dinner until tomorrow but I just happen to have blueberry muffins in the oven. Would you like room service tonight?"

"Sounds great." Blueberry muffins were her favorite kind.

"We might even let you open your gifts in bed."

As her mother turned to leave, Willow said, "Wait a minute, Mom."

Her mother looked back.

Willow tried to keep her voice casual, as if this question were perfectly ordinary. "Do you remember if I made a drawing for Grandma once, for a present? It was a red picture on yellow paper, when I was real little."

"It was for Mother's Day," Mrs. Paige said, "when you were three. You knew it was Mother's Day because Dad took you and Sarah shopping the day before. He bought gifts for me and for Grandma. But you made the drawing all on your own and when Grandma and Grandpa came for dinner that day, you brought it to her, so proud, and you said, 'Happy . . .' and then you stopped. You couldn't remember what the occasion was. Finally you blurted out, 'Happy YOUR Day!' and handed her the drawing. I'll never forget it."

Mrs. Paige's eyes looked moist. "Mother never forgot it, either. She kept that drawing and I found it in her desk, when I went through her things."

"What did you do with it?"

"I couldn't bear to throw it out; I put it in your Save Box."

"Could I see it?"

Mrs. Paige went into the hall and opened the linen closet. From her bed, Willow saw her mother reach up to the top shelf and remove a brown cardboard box. She carried it back to Willow's room and handed it to her.

The box was labeled *Willow's Save Box* and it contained items such as report cards, school pictures, and her Certificate of Graduation from Tiny Tots Nursery School. There were some old newspaper clippings and the book of poetry that Willow's fifth grade class put together and a pile of other keepsakes. Her mother rummaged through it all and handed her a piece of yellow construction paper, covered with red squiggles and lines. On the back was written, "Happy YOUR Day from Willow, age 3." She recognized her grandmother's handwriting.

Willow stared at the drawing. It was exactly what she'd seen in her mind as she struggled to keep her head above the water at Pinecone Lake. Apparently she had recalled, in accurate detail, a scene from her childhood, a scene which she had consciously forgotten.

And the other scene? Did that, too, come from some vast subconsciousness?

Only one explanation made any sense. She'd heard that

when people are near death, important scenes from their lifetimes sometimes flash before their eyes. This would explain the Mother's Day scene with her grandparents, and Willow's knowledge that she was loved.

But what about the other scene? The odd clothing, the raft made from branches, and the river with tall reeds and crocodiles, unlike any river Willow knew?

Was it possible that scenes from a previous lifetime might also flash before one's eyes, just before death? Had she lived before, long ago in another time and place? And had the girl with the braid lived then, too?

Did the same person save her from drowning twice—once when she was Willow Paige and once when she was someone named Kalos? Kalos who? She didn't know that other person's last name. The girl who floundered in the river reeds had no identity except, inexplicably, the name Kalos.

It was enough.

I was Kalos, Willow thought. She didn't know how or why, but she knew she had witnessed herself in another body.

Where had it been? When?

"Are you sure you're all right?" Mrs. Paige asked. "You look a bit pale."

Willow forced a smile.

"What made you ask about this drawing? I'm surprised you even remember it."

"I didn't exactly remember it," Willow said. "I . . ." She hesitated. Should she tell her mother what had happened? Should she describe the scenes and explain her certainty that the people in the second one were herself and the girl with the braid, even though the scene clearly took place long ago, in a far-off country?

Maybe she should. Maybe Mom could help her understand what it all meant.

"It happened while I was in the water," Willow said. "Just before . . ."

In the kitchen, the oven timer buzzed loudly.

"Excuse me, Willow," her mother said. "The muffins are done. I'll be back with your dinner in a few minutes."

Willow dropped the squiggly red drawing back into the carton labeled *Willow's Save Box* and watched her mother hurry from the room.

$$\boxed{3}$$

THAT NIGHT, she dreamed about Kalos and Tiy.

Her parents came into her room to say goodnight, the way they used to when she was little.

"You gave us a scare," Mr. Paige said.

"I don't even want to think about it," Mrs. Paige said. "If we lost you. . . ."

"We didn't lose her," Mr. Paige said. "And we aren't going to." He spoke firmly, as if by speaking with assurance, Fate would not dare to prove him wrong. "Happy birthday, Willow. And many happy returns."

Many happy returns. As she thought of Kalos and Tiy, the traditional birthday greeting took on a new meaning.

She heard the "click" of the bedside lamp and she heard her parents leave the room. Then she fell into a deep sleep, and had the first of the dreams.

Kalos was walking with her family—her mother, father, and Tiy—on a dirt road. Kalos and her mother and Tiy all wore long white linen gowns, belted at the waists. Her father wore a white loin cloth, crossed in front. Other people, similarly attired, walked near them but nobody spoke. It was early in the morning, not yet dawn. The round moon cast a silvery sheen on the road as they walked toward the temple of Amun-Ra, to worship.

Of all the gods, Kalos loved Amun-Ra the best. And of all the holy days, this was her favorite. Even though it meant getting up from her sleeping mat long before it was light and making the long walk to the temple of Amun-Ra, Kalos didn't mind. She hoped they would arrive early enough to get a good vantage point.

The temple was designed so that at dawn on the day of the winter solstice, the sun's rays shone directly on the temple altar. Kalos got gooseflesh on her arms, just thinking about it. Of course, she could never see the altar itself; only the priests were allowed inside the temple. But on this special morning, devout people gathered outside the temple and waited to see if Amun-Ra would ascend on time.

Last year, Kalos had been close enough to hear the chanting of the priests and her heart had filled with joy when Amun-Ra's glorious light arrived. Since then, the season of sowing and the season of harvest had passed, and now, today, the earth was again in exactly the right position.

She thought the people who designed the temple were the most clever people in the land. Surely Amun-Ra would reward them generously.

Kalos set her basket of grapes, pomegranates, and duck

eggs with the other offerings. Then she stood outside the dark temple, huddled shoulder to shoulder with other people from the village, waiting for Amun-Ra to illuminate the sky. It made her shiver with excitement to know that this was the exact moment when winter began.

Shortly before dawn, her father began the solemn prayers.

"Thou art beautiful, O gleaming Amun-Ra.

When thou risest in the east, thy warmth spreads across all the land and chases the darkness away.

Thou art mighty. Thou art high and shining. Thy rays sparkle on the mountaintops and penetrate the deepest sea.

We praise thee, mighty Amun-Ra, king of the gods, giver of all life."

Kalos felt a special love for Amun-Ra. The other gods were only names, faraway deities with no visible form. Amun-Ra was real. She could look up whenever she chose and see his sun-boat sailing across the sky. Whenever she felt the heat of the sun on her arms and face, she remembered that Amun-Ra had chosen her especially to receive his blessing. It was a secret she had shared with no one.

As the prayer continued, she looked upward. Would Amun-Ra bless them again this year? She had worshipped him faithfully and loved him truly. Her family had never taken water from a neighbor's field, nor baked sacrificial loaves that were too small. Still, the gods were sometimes unpredictable and there was always the chance that she would stand here in the darkness, past the time of dawning, while Amun-Ra stayed hidden in the chambers of the underworld, sailing his boat along the river-under-the-Earth.

In the darkness, something touched her hand. It was Tiy. Tiy's fingers trembled as they intertwined with hers and Kalos knew her sister shared her apprehension. Kalos squeezed Tiy's hand, to reassure her, and Tiy squeezed back. The firm pressure of her sister's hand made Kalos stand straighter.

Slowly, the sky lightened. She could make out the shadowy forms of the date palm trees and, beyond them, the temple's great pylon.

The ram-headed sphinxes along the road went from gray to silver to pink as the morning's first light touched them. And then, in a sudden glowing burst of brightness, the golden rays of Amun-Ra shone directly on the temple's massive columns. Winter was here but they need not fear its darkness, for once again Amun-Ra promised heat and light in abundance.

Kalos closed her eyes and felt the light of Amun-Ra surround her, enter her, shine through her. Her heart filled with love for this most wonderful of gods. She knew Amun-Ra had chosen her, more than the others, to receive his special light. When she felt it shining through her, she was filled with gladness.

WILLOW AWOKE with a start. Her heart pounded and she felt an incredible sense of well-being. She blinked in the darkness, unsure at first where she was. Gradually, she realized she was in her own room, in the same bed she'd slept in every night since she was two years old.

She closed her eyes and tried to recall the dream which made her feel so happy.

Tiy. The name leapt into Willow's mind and with it, the dream came back to her. She saw herself as Kalos, with her family, at the temple. She felt again her love and gratitude toward Amun-Ra.

Amun-Ra! Willow had never heard of any god named Amun-Ra. And she'd never had strange dreams like that before, dreams peopled with herself in a different body, living in a distant, unknown land.

The odd dream made Willow anxious. Was it possible that the near-drowning had somehow affected her brain? Was she hallucinating? Was the scene of Kalos falling from the raft and now the dream of Kalos outside the temple some bizarre trick of her mind?

Or was she actually recalling scenes from a previous lifetime?

Maybe when she was drowning, the scene from an earlier lifetime came to her and now, even though she was no longer in any danger, the way was somehow cleared for more of those long ago memories to surface.

The thought excited and scared her at the same time. Was it dangerous to have such dreams? Was it possible for her to slip backwards in time and not return?

Again, she wished she knew the identity of the girl with the braid. She remembered the piercing look the girl gave her as Willow watched her struggle with the beach umbrella. At the time, Willow thought it was because the girl had caught her staring. Now she wondered if it was something more. Had the girl with the braid recognized Willow? Was the girl already aware of a kinship in another life?

I need to find her, Willow thought. I need to find out

whether she knows anything about a previous life. If I don't, I'll always wonder about this.

At breakfast the next morning, Willow said, "I'd really like to find the girl who saved me from drowning. I want to thank her in person."

"Why don't you look in your school yearbook?" suggested Mr. Paige. "If she was at Pinecone Lake, she probably lives somewhere in this area."

After Willow loaded the dishes into the dishwasher, she took out her yearbook and looked carefully at every picture. None of them looked anything like the girl with the braid. She described the girl to Sarah, too, but Sarah had no idea who it might be.

"Could I put a notice in the newspaper?" Willow asked. "In the Personals column?"

Willow and Gretchen read the Personals faithfully. There were always several ads describing the kind of person the ad-placer wanted to date.

Young athletic nonsmoking male wishes to meet attractive woman under 30. Purpose: tennis, sailing, and ?

Willow and Gretchen wrote fake responses to the ads, describing themselves in glowing terms and adding ten years to their ages. *Dear Sir: I am a gorgeous gymnastics instructor, age 23. I like tennis and sailing; I love ?* They never mailed such letters, of course, but they had fun writing them.

Mr. Paige agreed that an ad would be Willow's best chance to locate the girl.

Willow composed the ad carefully. She wanted to put in something about a past life but she was afraid she'd sound so crazy that the girl with the braid wouldn't answer the ad, even if she saw it. She decided to find the girl first and then worry about whether they had known each other before, in another lifetime.

Will girl who saved other girl from drowning on August 23 at Pinecone Lake please call 344–6005?

"I don't like putting our telephone number in the newspaper," Mrs. Paige said. "We could get all manner of crazy calls."

"Would you rather have me put in our address?" Willow asked.

"No. That's even worse."

"She has to have some way to contact me."

Willow knew why her mother hesitated. When Sarah first got sick, the local paper did a story about her. It told how cheerful she was and how determined to fight her disease and win. On the day the article was printed, the Paiges received several telephone calls. Most were from other people who knew a leukemia patient. Most offered sympathy or advice. But one of the calls was terrible.

Willow had answered it. A man's voice, scratchy and low, had whispered, "Sarah's going to die. Sarah's going to die soon and the worms will eat her body."

Horrified, Willow had handed the phone to her father. Mr. Paige listened for a moment, cursed, and hung up. The man didn't call back but for weeks afterwards, whenever the phone rang, Willow remembered his sinister voice, whispering in her ear. She still shuddered, every time she thought about it.

Willow agreed; she didn't want a phone number in the ad.

"Let's rent a Post Office box," Mr. Paige suggested. "We can use the box number in the ad."

"Great idea," Willow said. "If any weird people read the ad, they won't know where we live or our phone number."

Mrs. Paige nodded her agreement. Mr. Paige said he would stop at the Post Office on his lunch hour and rent the box. Then he would call the newspaper and place the ad.

That afternoon, Willow went back to Pinecone Lake. She didn't swim. She walked along the beach and looked at the people. For awhile she sat in the sun, relishing the warmth on her shoulders. She closed her eyes and turned her face up. As always, the sun soothed her.

Thank you, Amun-Ra, she thought and smiled to herself. She liked having this new—or was it old?—name for the sun. She wondered if her fondness for the sun had anything to do with the feelings of Kalos. Was this part of her personality a carry-over from that earlier existence? Did she, Willow, like the warmth of the sun so much because in another lifetime she had worshipped a sun god?

Willow stood up and began walking again. The more she thought about the whole situation, the more complicated it became. Was reincarnation possible? Do people live more than one life? If they do, how soon does it happen? Are they born again right away or do many years go by in between lives?

Maybe Grandma and Grandpa had already been reborn. What if some little baby, yowling and sucking on a bottle, was Grandma? That idea gave her a creepy feeling. And it didn't fit with the fact that, when she was drowning, she saw Grandma and Grandpa waiting for her. They held out their arms to her, looking just the way they used to look.

Maybe she should forget the whole thing. Put Kalos and Tiy and the girl with the braid completely out of her mind and pretend that none of this had ever happened.

Only she couldn't. She was too curious; the vision and the dream had seemed too real. She continued down the beach, searching for the girl with the braid.

The girl with the braid was not there.

4

THE AMBULANCE came at midnight.

Two days after Willow's birthday, Sarah awoke in the night, drenched with sweat. She complained of pain in her knees and elbows. Mrs. Paige took Sarah's temperature, looked at the thermometer, and called Dr. Rogers immediately.

"It's probably only the flu," Sarah protested. "Let's wait and see how I feel tomorrow. I'll take Tylenol."

Willow could tell by looking at Sarah that it was not the flu. Sarah was pale as a new moon in winter and there were odd red blotches on her arms. She needed more than Tylenol. Much more.

"Call an ambulance," Dr. Rogers said. "I'll meet you at the hospital."

Willow felt sick herself as she watched the attendants wheel Sarah toward the door.

"We'll follow you in our car," Mr. Paige said, "and meet you at the emergency entrance." He turned to Willow. "Can you hold down the fort here by yourself?" he asked.

Willow nodded.

"We'll call you when we know anything," Mr. Paige said, and then they were gone.

Willow stood at the living room window and watched the whirling ambulance lights and the red taillights of her parents' car disappear. She turned on the TV. She might as well watch an old movie; there was no way she could sleep.

She wanted to call Gretchen and ask if Gretchen could come over, but she knew Gretchen's parents would not let her go out alone after midnight nor would they want to get up and drive her over.

At 3 A.M., she made buttered popcorn and shared it with Muttsie. At 4:30, she fell asleep on the sofa. That's where she was when her parents came home, just after nine.

"They gave her a transfusion," Mrs. Paige said.

That didn't tell her much. Sarah often had transfusions.

"How long will she have to stay?" Willow asked.

"We don't know. You can visit her this afternoon." Mrs. Paige spoke slowly, as if it were an effort to form the words. Her voice sounded raspy, like a bad long-distance telephone connection. "At least we have insurance that covers all of this," she said. "And we live near a fine cancer hospital. Some people have to travel hundreds of miles to get expert care like Sarah's getting."

Willow realized her mother was trying not to cry. Probably it was easier for her to talk about the insurance and the hospital than about Sarah.

* * *

THAT AFTERNOON, Willow rode her bike to the hospital, as she had done so many times the year before, and signed in at the visitors' station. Sarah was in the Intensive Care Unit.

Willow tried not to look at the patients she passed on her way to Sarah's room, but it was impossible not to hear when a loud moan echoed down the hall. An older couple in drab outdated clothing stood at the nurses' station; the woman clutched the man's sleeve, crying silently.

"Sarah?" Willow whispered, unsure whether Sarah was asleep or awake.

Sarah's eyes fluttered open.

"I have to talk fast," Willow said. "I only get to stay fifteen minutes."

Sarah blinked but said nothing. Willow swallowed. She hated trying to carry on a normal conversation when nothing about the situation was normal. Nothing.

"I saw Pete Wellington this morning," she said.

Pete Wellington was in Sarah's grade and Sarah had secretly had a crush on him ever since Willow could remember. On her way to the hospital, Willow had made a special trip to Burger King, where Pete worked, so she could report to Sarah.

"He said to tell you he says 'hi'."

In truth, Pete had acted like he didn't know who Willow was. When Willow said, "I'll tell her 'hi' from you, if you want me to," Pete had mumbled, "Huh? Oh. OK."

But Willow was not going to tell Sarah that. Sarah needed something cheerful, not something depressing. "I think he likes you, Sarah," she said. "I'll bet anything he asks you to go to the Homecoming Dance with him this fall."

Willow watched Sarah's expression carefully. If *that* didn't get a reaction, her sister was really sick. Sarah's lips curved slightly and Willow continued, in a rush. "If Pete does ask you to the dance, let's experiment with your hair. Maybe you could wear it pulled back, with one of those big, flat bows. Or swept to one side. Something sophisticated. Something that will make you irresistible."

Before she got sick, Sarah's hair was her best feature. It was thick and shiny, cascading to her shoulders in natural waves. She never had to get a perm or do anything to it except shampoo and brush it. Last year, while she was having the chemotherapy, Sarah's hair fell out and she had to wear a wig. It was a nice wig but Sarah hated it and Willow didn't blame her.

When Sarah was in remission, her hair grew back. It wasn't shoulder length but it was as thick and wavy as ever.

Willow stopped talking when she saw tears in Sarah's eyes.

"What's wrong?" she asked.

"I have to have more chemotherapy," Sarah said.

That's all she said but Willow knew what she was thinking. More chemotherapy could mean only one thing. The remission was over. The leukemia was back.

Willow remembered how sick the chemotherapy treatments had made Sarah. How could she endure the nausea again? And her hair—what if all her hair fell out again? How could she stand it?

"Oh, Sarah Peony," Willow said, instinctively using the old nickname. "I'm sorry."

Both Sarah and Willow loved flowers. One summer when they were small, the girls each chose a favorite flower and announced that they were changing their middle names.

"My name is Willow Sweet Pea," Willow had declared.

"And I am Sarah Peony," Sarah said.

For a few weeks, they refused to answer anyone who failed to call them Willow Sweet Pea and Sarah Peony.

Then one day, Sarah Peony burst into tears when she discovered that her beloved peonies were done blooming for that year, while the sweet peas would produce flowers all summer. She continued to sob, even when Grandma told her that peonies are perennials.

"They come up year after year," Grandma said. "They die back in the fall but every spring, they grow again, green and sturdy, and produce beautiful blossoms. Sweet peas must be seeded again each year but peonies renew themselves."

Sarah refused to be comforted.

After that, the girls were Willow and Sarah again but occasionally one of the old flower names popped out, a reminder of more carefree times.

Willow reached for Sarah's hand and pressed it.

"You'll get through it," Willow said. "You did before. Maybe it isn't as bad the second time. And maybe the next remission will last longer. Like about fifty years."

Sarah didn't smile at the feeble joke. She just looked at Willow and, for the first time since Sarah got sick, Willow saw defeat on her sister's face.

Mrs. Paige asked for a leave of absence from work. She spent all day at the hospital and Mr. Paige went directly there after work. They ate dinner in the hospital cafeteria.

When Willow joined them, she felt invisible. The whole meal went by and no one asked what Willow had done that day.

The next day she fixed her own dinner at home: a peanut butter and banana sandwich. She knew how to cook spaghetti and tuna casserole and she baked great blueberry muffins but all of those seemed like too much trouble, just for herself.

With Sarah away, the house felt empty. There was no one to talk to or watch TV with. Willow wouldn't mind getting Sarah a drink or helping Sarah into the bathtub. She wouldn't mind at all.

She dusted Sarah's room and put a red ribbon on Herbert, Sarah's stuffed toy buffalo. Finally she took Muttsie out in the backyard.

It was a warm night and the new neighbor, Mrs. Clauson, had her windows open. Willow didn't mean to eavesdrop; she couldn't avoid hearing Mrs. Clauson's voice over the fence.

Mrs. Clauson had moved in two weeks earlier. She was a plump, gray-haired woman who boarded pets, to bring in a little extra money. "It supplements my Social Security," she explained, when the Paiges went over to welcome her to the neighborhood. "And I enjoy the animals."

That day, her voice had been warm and bubbly. Willow had fancied that Mrs. Clauson was Santa Claus in disguise. Now, as Willow stood outside with Muttsie, Mrs. Clauson sounded more like the Wicked Witch of the West.

"Is this the party who's offering a reward for a white poodle?" Pause. "I think I have your dog. Can you describe him?" Another pause. "Yes, that's him. I found him this morning. One hundred dollars doesn't seem like very much reward for such a fine dog. I think he is worth two hundred."

Willow frowned. Once she and her father found a panicky collie running along the highway, its tongue hanging down like an untied shoelace. They stopped, coaxed the dog into their car, and brought it home. When the collie's owner offered them a reward, Mr. Paige had refused to take it. He said he was glad to help.

But Mrs. Clauson was negotiating for more money before she returned the poodle to its owner. Great, Willow thought. Our kindly, animal-loving neighbor is a greedy hypocrite.

"I'll meet you in the parking lot of the Broadmoore Shopping Center in an hour," Mrs. Clauson said. "Bring cash."

Apparently, the poodle's owner had agreed to pay the larger reward.

Completely disgusted, Willow took Muttsie back inside. She didn't want to watch while Mrs. Clauson put the poodle in her car.

5

TOGAS. Maybe the long white gowns were Roman togas.

History was not Willow's best subject. She never got the history questions right when she played Trivial Pursuit but she did remember pictures of people in togas. If she read about Rome, she might find something to prove that her dream was a memory, not an overactive imagination. And a trip to the library would take her mind off Sarah.

She found three books with chapters on Roman gods. Jupiter was the main god and Willow recognized the names of Mars and Diana. There was no mention of Amun-Ra.

One book had drawings of people in ancient Rome. Their togas were long and white, but they were different from the gowns in her dream.

Discouraged, she went home. No one was there.

Willow wandered restlessly from room to room. She tried

to call Gretchen but there was no answer. She looked in the refrigerator. There was sandwich meat and cheese and lettuce. There was blackberry yogurt and half a jar of spaghetti sauce. Nothing sounded good. It seemed like too much trouble to make a sandwich or cook spaghetti. Instead, she ate an entire package of Oreo cookies and drank two glasses of milk. Then she felt sick to her stomach.

She decided to go for a walk. Maybe some fresh air would make her feel better. As she started down the sidewalk, she saw Mrs. Clauson trying to coax a cocker spaniel from her car. Mrs. Clauson tugged on the leash but the dog refused to budge.

When Mrs. Clauson saw Willow, she smiled and said, "I seem to have a reluctant boarder. I can't understand it. The last time Jericho stayed with me, he made himself right at home. Now he won't get out of the car."

Willow went over to the car and held out her hand for the dog to sniff. "Good Jericho," she said. "Good dog."

The cocker spaniel's tail thumped against the seat of Mrs. Clauson's car.

"Come, Jericho," Willow said. "Come here."

To her surprise, the dog jumped down. When Mrs. Clauson pulled on the leash, Jericho trotted after her toward the house.

"You certainly have a way with dogs," Mrs. Clauson said. "I may have to make you a partner in my boarding business."

Willow started to mention the white poodle that Mrs. Clauson had found. Then she realized that she knew about it from overhearing Mrs. Clauson's conversation. She didn't want Mrs. Clauson to think she went sneaking around at night, listening at windows, so she didn't say anything about the poodle.

That night, she was invited to eat dinner and spend the night with Gretchen. Dinner was baked chicken and potato salad and a creamy casserole of peas and onions. Willow had two helpings of everything. While they ate, Gretchen's little brother, Ryan, told a series of "knock-knock" jokes that he'd learned at camp. Willow and Gretchen moaned and rolled their eyes at the corny jokes.

Later they sat in Gretchen's room and painted their toenails with Gretchen's new polish, "Flaming Flamingo."

"Have you ever thought about what happens to us after we die?" Willow asked.

"If you've been saved, your soul goes to Heaven."

Gretchen went to church twice a week and was sure that what she learned there was true. Willow was never so certain.

"I mean later," Willow said. "Do you think a human soul could come back to earth again, maybe hundreds of years later, in a different body?"

"You mean reincarnation?"

"Yes."

"My pastor says talk of reincarnation is The Devil speaking."

"Why? What would be evil about living more than once? Maybe the second time we'd do better."

"If you're in Heaven, living with Jesus, why would you want to come back to earth?"

"I don't know."

"Believe me, you would not want to be reincarnated."

Willow didn't say anything more. She knew from expe-

34

rience that there was no use arguing with Gretchen when it came to the teachings of Gretchen's church. Once when Willow told Gretchen that she didn't believe there was a devil, Gretchen said such talk was only proof that there *is* a devil and that he was speaking through Willow.

Willow sometimes envied Gretchen her certainty that she had the answers to all of life's questions. It must be comforting to feel so sure. Still, Willow could not help questioning Gretchen's beliefs and she decided not to tell Gretchen that she thought she was once a girl named Kalos.

When Willow got to the hospital the next afternoon, Sarah had been transferred out of ICU to a regular ward. She found the new room number and went in.

Her mother was sitting in a chair, doing the crossword puzzle from the morning paper. "I'm glad you're here," Mrs. Paige said. "You can stay with Sarah while I go get some lunch."

Willow stood beside Sarah's bed. Her sister's skin had a bluish tinge and there were dark circles under her eyes.

"I hope you are ready to laugh," Willow said, "because I am here with a brand new comedy routine, straight from Cub Scout Camp." Corny jokes were better than nothing.

Mrs. Paige gave Willow a grateful look and left the room.

Sarah looked at Willow. She didn't smile.

"Here we go," Willow said. "Knock. Knock."

Sarah closed her eyes.

"Come on, Sarah," Willow said. "This first one's pretty funny. Knock. Knock."

Sarah lay still.

Willow hesitated. Then she repeated, "Knock. Knock,"

35

and in a different, higher voice, said, "Who's there?" She finished the joke, doing both parts herself. "Police." "Police who?" "Police get well soon." She clasped her hands together, as if she were begging. "Pretty police."

Sarah watched her soberly. She didn't smile. She didn't roll her eyes. She didn't respond at all.

Willow took a deep breath. "OK," she said. "It wasn't the greatest joke in the world. But it wasn't *that* bad, was it?"

"I'm going to die," Sarah said.

Willow's smile faded.

"They think I don't know," Sarah went on. "The doctors and Mom and Dad all pretend that I'm getting better but it isn't true. I'm dying. I can feel it."

"How can you be so sure? Did you ask?"

"If I ask, they'll cover up the truth. They think I can't handle it. You're the only one I can be honest with."

Willow didn't know what to say. When Sarah was so sick last time, she kept saying she wouldn't let leukemia beat her, that she would fight until she won. The doctors had said her remission was due at least in part to Sarah's will to live.

"You can't give up," Willow said. "You have to try to get well."

Sarah closed her eyes again. "It's no use," she said. "I've already tried. It didn't work."

"Maybe this time will be different. The remission might last longer. If you can fight it long enough, someone will discover a cure."

Sarah shook her head. "I'm too tired," she said. "I don't want to fight it any longer." A tear trickled down her cheek.

Willow bit her lip and struggled to hold back her tears.

She felt helpless. What could she say? What could she do for her sister?

As she stood by Sarah's bed, she remembered her own panic, when she thought she was drowning. And she remembered how the love of her grandmother, and of Tiy, had filled her with peace.

She reached out and took Sarah's hand in hers. She didn't say anything; she just squeezed Sarah's hand. When Sarah opened her eyes, Willow smiled at her. The feelings of love that went through her hand and into Sarah were electrical. She felt them in her fingertips and she was sure Sarah felt them, too.

For the first time that day, Sarah smiled. Willow squeezed Sarah's hand and Sarah squeezed back. Then Sarah closed her eyes and, still smiling, fell asleep.

After she left the hospital, Willow stopped at the Post Office, as she did every afternoon, and checked to see if there was a letter for her in the P.O. box. There was none.

As the days went by, the chance that she would find the girl with the braid grew slim. Willow thought about her less often. The memories of Kalos came less frequently, too.

Willow wondered what the girl with the braid would say if she knew what Willow wanted. Would she think Willow was crazy to talk about being sisters in another lifetime? Would the girl be like Gretchen and think the whole idea was sinful?

When Willow thought about reincarnation, she found the idea comforting. If she had lived before, it was logical to think she would live again; she would have another life after this one.

And if she would live again, so would Sarah. No matter

what happened in Sarah's battle against leukemia, this lifetime would not be the end for her.

She wondered if she should tell Sarah what had happened. Tell her about the vision when Willow was drowning, and about the dream. She could tell Sarah how she saw Grandma and Grandpa waiting for her. Maybe it would help Sarah to know that even if she died, it wasn't the end of everything. Maybe she really would get to see Grandma and Grandpa again. Who knows? Maybe Willow and Sarah would be sisters again sometime.

Or was she indulging in wishful thinking? Maybe this whole business about another life had happened because her subconscious mind was worried about Sarah. Because she was thinking about Sarah so much and about what would happen if Sarah died, perhaps her mind had conjured up this image of a past life, as a way to soothe Willow's fears.

After all, she had no evidence of any past life. There was no tape recording of herself speaking as Kalos. She had never talked to one of the psychics who claimed to lead people into past-life regressions.

Her belief that she lived before was based solely on the vision that flashed before her eyes when she was drowning, and the dream which came that same night. Flimsy evidence, her father would say.

And yet, Willow knew that feelings were sometimes more important than facts. She had learned long ago to trust her instincts, to judge people by how she felt about them rather than by what facts she knew about them.

On the other hand, she didn't want to mislead Sarah or

to sound like Gretchen's mother. Once when Mrs. Bremmer came to pick up Gretchen from Willow's house, she told Sarah, "Trust God's will, my dear. If He takes you soon, it means you're going to be with Jesus for all eternity."

"We hope to have Sarah stay here with us awhile longer," Mrs. Paige said.

"But it might not be God's will," Mrs. Bremmer said. "God loves us and He decides everything that should happen to us."

Willow remembered how her mother's eyes had flashed as she responded, "I cannot believe that God specifically chose Sarah to have this terrible disease."

After Mrs. Bremmer left, Mrs. Paige said, "I didn't mean to offend her. But she thinks she has an easy answer for our problem when there are no easy answers."

Willow wondered if a belief in reincarnation was another easy answer to a difficult question. She decided not to say anything to Sarah about the vision and the dream. Not yet.

The next day, the letter arrived. Willow stared at the glass door of the Post Office box for a moment and then double-checked the box number, to be sure it was correct.

She slit the envelope open and read the letter right there, while she stood in the Post Office.

To whom it may concern:

I think I'm the person you're looking for. On August 23, my cousin and I went to Pinecone Lake and while I was there, I saw a girl go under more than once so I swam out and pulled her to shore. Later, her mother came and took her to the doctor.

My name is Helen Granston and I'm 13 years old.

Willow stopped reading and recalled the face and eyes of the girl with the braid. Helen. Her name was Helen. It seemed to fit.

I live in San Francisco, the letter said. No wonder her picture was not in the Bellefield School yearbook. *I'm visiting my cousin until September 4. You can call me there.* A phone number and signature were at the bottom of the page.

Willow tucked the letter in her pocket and headed home. September 4 was only two days away. She hoped she would be able to meet Helen before Helen went home. Willow couldn't imagine bringing up the subject of a past life together in a telephone call. It would have to be done in person, after she and Helen got to know each other better.

Before she made the call, she practiced what she would say. She was afraid if she didn't, she would get excited and start to babble and then Helen would decide she didn't want to meet Willow, after all.

She didn't babble. When Helen answered, Willow gave her name and said she'd received the letter.

"My aunt saw your ad in the paper," Helen said. "I knew it had to be me. I mean, good grief, there couldn't be two people who almost drowned on the same day, in the same lake, could there now? So I'm the one you're looking for."

"Do you have long blonde hair?" Willow asked. "And you wear it . . ."

"In a braid."

"You're the one."

They decided to meet at 3 P.M. the next day at McDonald's. It was close to where Helen was staying and it wasn't far from the hospital. Willow could go to visit Sarah and then meet Helen afterwards.

She took extra care with her appearance the next day. The only time Helen had seen Willow up close, Willow was vomiting into the sand. She hoped to make a better impression this time.

She didn't want to overdo it by getting all dressed up but she wore her good jeans and her blue sweater, the one that made her eyes look wider and bluer.

She was almost ready to leave when Gretchen called.

"Do you want to come over this afternoon?" Gretchen asked. "We can listen to my albums and make brownies."

"I can't. I'm going to visit Sarah."

"Come afterwards. Mom says its OK if you stay for dinner. Maybe we can talk my dad into renting a video."

"I can't today. I—I'm meeting someone."

"You sound awfully mysterious. Is the someone tall, dark, and good looking?"

"Hardly. I'm meeting the girl who rescued me at the lake."

"You found her? That's great! How did you . . ."

"I'll tell you about it later, Gretchen. I have to go now."

She hadn't intended to tell anyone about Helen until after they met. There wasn't any reason to keep it a secret; she just didn't feel like talking about it.

When she got to the hospital, Sarah was asleep. Willow sat by Sarah's bed anyway. Maybe Sarah would sense her presence.

She told her mother that she was going to McDonald's on her way home.

Mrs. Paige looked guilty. "I'm sorry you've had to fend for yourself so much," she said.

"That's OK, Mom. Sarah needs you here."

"Yes." Mrs. Paige rubbed her eyes and Willow noticed the dark circles under them. "I want to have as much time with Sarah as I can," she said, "but unfortunately, that means I don't have time for anyone else. Not even you."

"That's OK," Willow repeated. "We'll have time together when Sarah gets better."

A shadow flickered across Mrs. Paige's face. She stood up and hugged Willow hard. Then she sat again beside Sarah's bed.

At 2:30, Willow punched the "Down" button on the hospital elevator and then ran down the stairs without waiting for the elevator to arrive. She didn't want to be late to McDonald's.

6

WILLOW ARRIVED first. She ordered French fries and carried them to the last booth in the back corner. She wanted to talk to Helen with as few distractions as possible.

She dunked a French fry into the catsup and nibbled it. She was too nervous to be hungry but she needed to do something with her hands. What would she say to Helen?

Helen came in and looked around. Willow waved at her; Helen waved back. She ordered a Coke before she joined Willow.

"Hi." They said the word exactly together and then laughed. Helen slid into the booth across from Willow.

They made small talk at first. Willow asked what school Helen's cousin went to and Helen said he went to a private school.

"Have you always lived in San Francisco?" Willow asked.

"No. My dad gets transferred a lot. We've lived all over the world—South America, Australia—even a year in Greece."

"It sounds exciting."

"It is, partly. But it's hard to be a foreigner and not know the language."

"Thanks for rescuing me that day," Willow said. "I would have drowned for sure, if you hadn't come after me."

"I'm glad I got there in time."

"How did you know I needed help? After I got the cramp, I tried to yell, but I didn't think any noise came out."

"I looked out at the water just as your head went under," Helen said. "Maybe it was mental telepathy."

Willow hesitated. If Helen believed in mental telepathy, maybe she knew something about reincarnation, too. Should she tell Helen about Kalos and Tiy? There might not be another opportunity and the worst that could happen would be that Helen would laugh at her and say the whole idea was crazy.

Willow took a deep breath and plunged in. "I had another reason for wanting to meet you," she said. "Something odd has happened to me—to us. It began when I was drowning, just as I felt myself lose consciousness."

She told every detail of the vision, how Tiy rescued Kalos from the crocodile and how she felt the love between Kalos and Tiy. She told about the dream, too, and the Temple of Amun-Ra.

She finished by saying, "When I rolled over in the sand that day and saw you looking at me, I believed you were Tiy."

"Good grief! Why would you think that? You said she had black hair."

"It isn't that you look like her; it's a *feeling*. I can't explain it very well because I don't understand it myself. I don't know why I thought that you were once Tiy. I just knew you were. And now that I'm with you again, I—I still think so. You were Tiy and I was Kalos. We were sisters, long ago."

As she spoke the words, Willow felt a chill tingle down her arms. It was true. When she looked at Helen, she experienced a bond too strong to be explained only by the fact that this girl had saved her from drowning. She would be grateful for that, no matter what sort of person Helen was. Willow felt far more than gratitude when she looked at Helen. She felt kinship. She felt love.

"Good grief!" Helen said. "Are you kidding?"

"No."

"This seems kind of flaky to me."

Willow tried not to look too disappointed. "I hope I can figure out where we were, and when, in that other life."

"You won't be able to prove we lived before, so why waste time trying?"

"I'm curious. I want to find out if there is a time and place in history when the things I saw in my mind might really have happened. At first, I thought the white robes were Roman togas but when I read about Rome, nothing sounded familiar or right."

"What about Greece? The Greeks wore white gowns, too. Or maybe it was one of the African countries. People always wear white in countries that are hot because white deflects the heat. Maybe Kalos and Tiy lived in Nigeria."

The more suggestions Helen made, the more discouraged Willow felt. Kalos and Tiy could have lived anywhere in the world and there were thousands of years of history to consider. It seemed impossible that she would ever prove anything.

"If you want my opinion," Helen said, "you should forget about your past and concentrate on the future."

Out loud, Willow agreed. But she knew she wouldn't give up the search for Kalos and Tiy so easily, no matter what Helen thought.

7

THE PHONE rang as Willow unlocked the door. It was Gretchen.

"Quick!" Gretchen said. "Get the paper and look at the Personals. There's an ad we have to answer."

Willow wasn't in the mood to write a fake letter but before she could say so, Gretchen bubbled on.

"This is the best one ever," Gretchen said. "I'll hold on while you find it."

Reluctantly, Willow got the newspaper and turned to the classified section.

"It's about halfway down in the Personals column," Gretchen said. "It begins: *Sixteen-year-old male seeking girl to date.*"

Willow ran her finger down the column. Before she found the ad Gretchen was talking about, she found one which interested her even more. It said, in capital letters, REINCARNATION.

Her finger stopped. Willow read the rest of the ad. *"Informative free seminar for anyone seeking spiritual answers. Sat., 9–1, in the Bellefield Library meeting room."*

"Do you see it?" Gretchen asked. "He sounds perfect for us. Believe me, we were meant to read the ads tonight. Maybe this time we'll even mail the letter."

"Yes," Willow said slowly. "Maybe you're right. Maybe we were meant to read the ads tonight."

"Can you believe a sixteen-year-old guy would place this ad? I hope he doesn't have acne."

Willow didn't reply. She was still staring at the ad which began, REINCARNATION. Perhaps this seminar would answer some of her questions.

"Willow? Are you still there?"

"I'm here."

"Do you want me to come over so we can write our answer now? We don't want a sixteen-year-old guy to slip through our fingers."

"I'm sorry, Gretchen. I don't feel much like writing an answer tonight. You go ahead without me."

"Oh." Willow heard the disappointment in Gretchen's voice. "I guess you're pretty worried about Sarah."

"Yes."

"I'll call you tomorrow then."

After she hung up, Willow sat staring at the newspaper. The announcement didn't say who was putting on the seminar. What if the people were weird? What if it was some kind of cult and they tried to get her to join?

The meeting would be at the public library, though. She was pretty sure that weird cults were not allowed to use the library's meeting room. And she could always get up and walk out if she didn't like the seminar.

On Saturday, Willow told her mother she was going to the library but she said nothing about the seminar. She knew her mother would assume that Willow wanted to check out some books to read. Mrs. Paige's mind was already in the hospital with Sarah; she didn't question Willow.

Willow was the only person in the meeting room who wasn't an adult but no one seemed to mind. The man at the door gave her a name tag and told her he was glad she came.

She sat down and glanced around. No one looked strange. They were just ordinary people. Most were about her parents' age; a few looked like they were sixty or older and there was one young couple who sat close together, holding hands.

The first speaker, Mr. Tyler, said, "Reincarnation is the process by which the eternal soul inhabits successive human bodies."

Willow wrote the definition in her notebook.

Mr. Tyler said many famous people believed in reincarnation. He read a list of names but the only ones Willow recognized were Henry David Thoreau and Benjamin Franklin.

Then he read several passages from the Bible and some things written by a man named Edgar Cayce. Willow wasn't too interested in the readings. Instead of listening, she reread the definition she'd written in her notebook. *Reincarnation is the process by which the eternal soul inhabits successive human bodies.*

If this were true, if it could really happen, then perhaps her soul and the soul of Kalos were the same. If one eternal soul could live in different human bodies, then maybe she had actually lived before and was now remembering that earlier life.

The second speaker was Mrs. Evans. She was young and pretty and she got Willow's attention right away.

"I'm going to speak," Mrs. Evans said, "about the five ways to recall past lives."

Willow leaned forward in her chair. She didn't want to miss anything.

"The most common way for an individual to regress to a past life," Mrs. Evans said, "is with the help of a therapist. It's a one-to-one situation and the results are usually good."

Willow wondered how people found such therapists. In the Yellow Pages? Listed under Reincarnation?

"The second way is for a group of people to recall past lives through the use of guided visualization."

Willow wrote *guided visualization* in her notebook.

"Third," Mrs. Evans continued, "a person sometimes has a special fondness for another time or place. Perhaps you care about a certain country, even though you have never been there. Or maybe you take a trip and when you arrive, you can find your way, without asking directions. You feel you've been there before."

Willow looked around. Other people were nodding in agreement.

A woman in the back spoke. "I collected Oriental art," she said, "long before I learned that I once lived in China."

"I went all over Paris," a man said, "without a map."

Willow felt discouraged. Did everyone else in the room know exactly what their past lives were? She did not have a special fondness for another country. She couldn't even figure out what country Kalos might have lived in, so how could she have any strong feelings for the place?

Maybe she was wrong. Maybe what she had thought was the memory of a past life wasn't really that at all.

"Are we born again right away?" someone asked.

"Sometimes. Or there might be centuries between lives."

Mrs. Evans glanced at her notes. "The other two ways to recall a past life are less common," she said. "One is spontaneous recall. When this happens, the memory of a past life appears one day out of the blue. Usually an entire scene will come to mind, full blown. Often, but not always, this happens during a time of stress."

Willow listened intently. Yes, she thought. That's what happened to me when I was drowning. She wrote *spontaneous recall* in her notebook.

"The last way that a past life can become known to us is through our dreams."

Willow held her breath. Mrs. Evans seemed to be looking straight at her.

"People sometimes dream about themselves in a different body, in a different time and place."

A man in the front row raised his hand. "I have lots of strange dreams," he said, "where I see myself as someone else. How do I know if what I've dreamed is really a scene from a past life? Maybe it's just my imagination or maybe a memory of something I've read in a book or seen in a movie. How do I prove it was another life?"

"It can't be proved scientifically," Mrs. Evans said. "The only proof is a sense of truth. Someone who has dreamed about a past life recalls the dream as if it were a real experience. It isn't a vague memory; it's full of specific details. When you dream about a past life, you know that what you saw in your dreams really happened to you. You *know* it."

Yes, Willow thought. *It really happened. All of it. Tiy and the crocodile. The Temple of Amun-Ra at sunrise.*

When the meeting ended, everyone was invited to stay for coffee. Willow stood up and started for the door. Before she could slip out, she felt a hand on her shoulder. Turning, she saw Mrs. Evans behind her.

"Did you like the seminar?" Mrs. Evans asked.

Willow nodded.

"When you came in, I thought you were probably just curious. Once we got some kids who came on a dare. They thought the whole seminar was a joke. I don't have much patience with people like that, who think reincarnation is all a hoax. But I watched you as I spoke. I saw the reaction in your eyes when I talked of seeing a past life in your dreams. You've had a dream like that, haven't you?"

"Yes."

"I thought so. Have you told anyone about it?"

"No."

"Not even your parents?"

"My parents have—other problems to think about."

"Divorce?"

"No. My sister's in the hospital. She has leukemia."

"I'm sorry. I hope she'll be all right."

Willow didn't answer.

"Was this seminar what you expected?" Mrs. Evans asked.

"I didn't know what to expect," Willow said, "but I learned a lot, especially from your speech."

"Good. I'm glad you came."

"Me, too. I was scared there was something wrong with me but now I know there isn't."

Mrs. Evans handed Willow a business card that had her name and telephone number on it. "If there's ever anything I can do to help you, please call me."

"Thanks." Willow tucked the card into her notebook and left the library.

The sky seemed bluer than it had when she entered. A cluster of yellow roses outside the library, the last until next summer, offered their faint, sweet scent as she passed. She hadn't noticed them when she went in but now she paused to sniff them, hugging her notebook as if it were a precious treasure.

She wasn't crazy. She had not been hallucinating or imagining. A group of logical, respectable adults believed that reincarnation was possible.

She *did* dream of a past life; she *did* see herself as Kalos. She wasn't worried anymore about finding proof.

"A sense of truth is the only proof," Mrs. Evans had said. A sense of truth.

Willow knew that her memories of Kalos and Tiy, and their life together, were true. She closed her eyes and lifted her face to the sun.

"Thank you, Amun-Ra," she said. Then she half-ran, half-skipped all the way home.

8

"SHE'S LOST her will to live."

Willow and her parents sat in the hospital cafeteria while Mrs. Paige reported what the doctor had said that morning.

"Dr. Rogers explained how he would do a bone marrow transplant if he can find a donor, and do you know what Sarah said? She said, 'Why bother? It won't work anyway.'" Mrs. Paige twisted her hands together. "The fight's gone out of her. It's as if she doesn't care whether she gets well or not."

"She's tired," Mr. Paige said. "It's hard to keep fighting when she's struggled for so long."

"We need to find something that would make her want to get well again. Something special, something for her to look forward to. Dr. Rogers says patients who try to get well do better than those who give up."

As she listened, Willow got an idea. She would get Pete

Wellington to visit Sarah and ask her to go out with him. Sarah would like that. A date with Pete would be something to look forward to.

Because of the risk of infection, Sarah was limited to one visitor per day, in addition to her parents. Usually, that visitor was Willow but if it would help Sarah to see Pete, Willow would give him her turn.

As soon as she and her parents finished lunch, she rode her bike over to Burger King and went inside. She was in luck. There were only two other customers and they already had their orders. She could talk to Pete alone.

"Hi, Pete," she said.

"Uh, hi." He looked surprised that she knew his name.

"I'm Willow Paige," she said. "Sarah Paige's sister."

"Oh," Pete said.

"Sarah's still in the hospital."

"Oh."

What a sparkling conversation, Willow thought. If Sarah ever does go out with Pete, I wonder what they'll talk about.

"I came to ask you to visit Sarah."

"Me?" Pete said.

"Yes." Who did he think she meant?

"At the hospital?"

Willow forced herself to keep smiling. "It would help her to have some company."

Pete looked away. "I'm not very good with sick people," he said. "Once when my sister cut her hand, I fainted."

"It would make Sarah feel better."

Pete still didn't look at her. Why was he making her beg? What was he so afraid of?

"Leukemia isn't contagious," Willow said, "if that's what you're wondering. And she doesn't look terrible. She isn't bleeding or anything like that and she's not hooked up to a bunch of tubes."

Pete glanced at the door, as if hoping a customer would come in and demand to be waited on. "I guess I ought to go see her," he said, "but . . . listen, tell her I'll come see her as soon as she gets home."

"You don't understand," Willow said. "Sarah is really sick. She—she may not go home."

Pete's eyes widened. "Are you telling me she's dying?" he asked. He wiped the palms of his hands across his pants. "Is that what you're saying?"

Willow glared at him. "I'm just saying we don't know if she'll get well or not. She'd like to see you. She needs something to look forward to and I thought you might ask her to go . . ."

"You want me to go see someone who's *dying*? Man, I can't handle that. No way. I'd faint for sure, if I had to look at someone who's dying."

Willow clenched her teeth and wondered what Sarah saw in this jerk. She'd like to bop him in the jaw, knock some sense into him. Instead, she smiled as sweetly as she could and said, "I promise you Sarah is still alive. If you go tomorrow, you'll be safe."

"The whole hospital scene gives me the creeps," Pete said. "Dying! Man, I didn't know Sarah was *that* sick."

Willow couldn't stand to hear any more. She spun around and marched out of Burger King. She would find some other way to help Sarah.

She didn't tell Sarah that she'd talked to Pete. What was the point? If Sarah got well, she'd find out soon enough what an idiot Pete was. And if Sarah didn't get well? In that case, Willow thought, it didn't matter about Pete.

She went back to the hospital and stood beside Sarah's bed. Sarah opened her eyes when Willow took her hand. Sarah's hand was frail as a soap bubble and Willow realized her sister had lost more weight.

"You're going to need a Size 3 soon," Willow said. "Maybe I should check in here and go on a diet, too."

Sarah smiled weakly. What am I doing? Willow thought. Sarah may not live through this and I stand here making stupid jokes about diets.

But she didn't know what else to say.

Sarah closed her eyes again and soon her breathing became deep and regular. Willow tiptoed out of the room.

She was supposed to meet Helen at McDonald's at six o'clock and she had to go home first to feed Muttsie and let him out.

"Why do you want to see me?" Helen had asked that morning, when Willow called her. "Did you have another one of your crazy dreams?"

"No. I have a present for you. A thank-you present." That was true, but it was only part of the reason why Willow wanted to see Helen again.

"I'm going home tomorrow morning," Helen said, "but I could meet you today, at McDonald's."

Willow got there right at six. She was afraid she was going to be late because Gretchen called just as Willow put Muttsie back in.

"Do you want to come over for dinner?" Gretchen asked. "My folks are going to a meeting and they said Ryan and I can send out for pizza."

If she told Gretchen she was going to McDonald's, Gretchen would want to go, too, and Willow wanted to be alone with Helen. They couldn't talk about reincarnation in front of Gretchen, not when Gretchen thought it was sinful.

"I can't come tonight," Willow said.

"Why not?"

"Mom likes me to be at the hospital as much as I can. I was just leaving." That wasn't a lie, even though she knew Gretchen would think she was leaving to go to the hospital.

She felt guilty for not telling Gretchen the truth. Gretchen would be hurt if she ever found out that Willow met Helen for a burger and didn't want to include Gretchen.

But this was her last chance to talk to Helen. Tomorrow morning, Helen would be gone. Willow could see Gretchen any time.

Helen liked her present, a thin silver bracelet.

While they ate, Willow told Helen about the seminar she'd gone to. "If I had the money," she said, "I'd pay a therapist to help me do a past-life regression. A professional could probably help me find out when and where we lived before."

"Maybe your parents will pay for it," Helen said. "Have you asked them?"

Willow shook her head. "They don't know anything about my dream or the visions I saw when I was drowning," she said. "You're the only one who knows. My parents are so worried about Sarah that I can't bother them with this."

"If they're anything like my parents, they wouldn't understand anyway," Helen said.

"Are you going to tell your parents about it?" Willow asked.

"What's there to tell? You're the one with the odd dreams, not me. I haven't seen any visions of myself in a different body."

Willow twisted a piece of hair around her finger. When Helen said it like that, the whole thing sounded crazy. Yet, she felt the same connection, the same strong bond with this girl, that she had felt before. Willow was more convinced than ever that Helen was once Tiy.

"I wish you didn't live so far away," Willow said. "Will you write to me?"

"I'm not much for writing letters. I always have good intentions but somehow I put it off."

"I can't afford long-distance calls." Willow looked down at her hands. Why was this so hard? She felt like she was saying good-bye to her dearest friend, instead of to a girl she'd met only twice before.

She was quiet for a moment, remembering how Helen had rescued her. A tingle of excitement shot down her back. She put her elbows on the table, leaned toward Helen and said, "When I was drowning, you knew I needed help, even though you didn't hear me. We communicated without words that day. Maybe we can do it again."

"You mean, you think we could talk somehow, without letters or phone calls?"

"Yes. If we try, maybe we can send our thoughts to each other." She knew her idea was farfetched, but what did she have to lose? She couldn't let Helen walk out of her life and never hear from her again.

"How would we do it?" Helen asked.

"What if," Willow said, "we set a time, the same time every day, and we agree to think of each other at exactly that time? That way our thoughts are specifically directed toward each other."

"Good grief," Helen said. "You have the most far-out ideas of anyone I ever met."

Willow wasn't sure if that was a criticism or a compliment. "At least I'm not boring," she said.

Helen laughed. "You are definitely not boring," she said. She put her elbows on the table and rested her chin on her hands. "I've always wondered if mental telepathy really works."

"Here's your chance to find out," Willow said. "We would both have to be alone when we do it. There couldn't be any distractions." She looked at Helen. "How about it? Do you want to try?"

"Why not? If it works, we can go on TV and make a million."

"What time should we set? When can you count on being by yourself?"

"How about five o'clock every afternoon?"

Five o'clock. Most days at five o'clock, Willow was home. During the school year, that's when she did her homework. In the summer, she usually watched the TV news or cooked something for dinner. Even now, with Sarah in the hospital, she could arrange to be home alone at five o'clock. Muttsie always had to be fed and taken out about that time.

"Five o'clock it is. We'll think of each other every day at

exactly five o'clock." Willow opened her wallet and took out a snapshot of herself. "Here," she said. "Maybe if you look at my picture at five o'clock, it will help you concentrate on me."

Helen tucked the snapshot into her shirt pocket. "I don't have a picture to give you," she said.

"Mail me one as soon as you get home. Can you start the mental telepathy tomorrow?"

"I guess so." Helen stood up and put her empty food containers on the tray.

"Tomorrow, then. Five o'clock sharp." It wasn't so hard to say good-bye to Helen now that she knew Helen would be thinking of her every single day at the same time. Maybe they would develop a mental telepathy that worked. Maybe they would actually be able to send their thoughts back and forth.

One thing was certain. It would be an interesting experiment. She could hardly wait until tomorrow, at five o'clock.

9

"I DIDN'T expect to see *you* here."

Willow jumped when she heard the familiar voice.

Gretchen stood just inside the door to McDonald's. "I thought you were going to the hospital," she said.

"My plans changed," Willow said. She introduced Helen to Gretchen. "I thought you were going to order pizza," she said.

"My plans changed, too."

Willow knew Gretchen was upset.

"I have to go," Helen said. "My aunt wants me to pack tonight. It was nice to meet you, Gretchen."

Willow put her hand on Helen's arm. "Good-bye, Tiy," she said softly. "I'll talk to you tomorrow."

"Yes," Helen said. "Tomorrow. Good-bye." Helen turned and walked out of McDonald's.

Willow swallowed and blinked hard. She wondered when —or if—she would see Helen again.

"What did you call her?" Gretchen said. "Tie?"

"Oh, that's just a nickname," Willow said.

"You two seem to know each other pretty well."

"Yes," Willow said. To herself she added, *Yes. We do know each other well. We lived together once in a mud house near the Nile River.*

As soon as she had the thought, her pulse quickened. The Nile River. It *was* the Nile River; she knew that somehow. She also knew that this one fact would make it much easier to figure out where Kalos and Tiy had lived. She rushed out the door of McDonald's, leaving Gretchen to stare after her.

"Wait!" Willow shouted. "I just thought of something!"

Helen turned back as Willow ran to catch up to her.

"It was the Nile River," Willow said. "That's where I had my raft, where the crocodile almost got me. You saved me from drowning in the Nile River."

"Good grief. How do you know that?"

"All of a sudden, the name just came to me."

Spontaneous recall, she thought, remembering what she had learned at the seminar. I know because of spontaneous recall.

"The Nile is in Africa," Helen said. "That will make it easier to find out about your sun god, won't it? Maybe he was one of the Egyptian gods."

Egypt. Yes, Willow thought, Kalos probably lived in ancient Egypt.

Impulsively, Willow hugged Helen. "Good-bye, sis," she said.

When Willow returned to McDonald's, Gretchen was gone.

As she pedaled home, Willow wished she had told Gretchen the truth from the start. Why hadn't she just said that she already had plans instead of letting Gretchen think that she was going to the hospital? She could have said that Helen had invited her to meet for dinner. That way, when Gretchen saw them together, she wouldn't have thought anything of it.

When she got home, she tried to call Gretchen. She let it ring twelve times before she hung up. Willow wondered if Gretchen was home and refusing to answer the phone.

The next day, Sarah was worse. Mr. Paige took the day off from work and stayed at the hospital. Willow and her mother stayed there, too. There wasn't anything they could do for Sarah but it seemed important to be there. At least Sarah knew she wasn't alone.

At four o'clock, Willow said she was going home to let Muttsie out. "I'll make something for our dinner," she said. She knew her parents would stay until visiting hours ended at eight.

Dinner and Muttsie were only excuses. She really wanted to be home at five o'clock, to be alone in the quiet house for her first experiment in mental telepathy.

She wondered exactly how it would work. Maybe she would get a vision of where Helen was and what she was doing. Or maybe Helen's message would suddenly appear in her mind, the way the name of the Nile River did.

When she got home, Gretchen was standing on the porch, holding a basket.

"My mother made a casserole for our dinner," she said, "and she made an extra for your family."

"Thanks," Willow said. "I was supposed to fix dinner and I don't feel like cooking."

"Mom called the hospital to find out when you would be home. Your mother said Sarah isn't doing too well. I'm sorry."

Willow unlocked the door and Gretchen followed her inside. Gretchen took the basket into the kitchen and put the casserole dish in the refrigerator.

"The instructions for baking it are taped on top," she said. "Can you believe how efficient my mother is?" She plopped down in a kitchen chair. "I've been petting Mrs. Clauson's current dog through the fence while I waited for you to get home. I've always liked cocker spaniels."

Willow glanced nervously at her watch. It was 4:45. Somehow she needed to get rid of Gretchen in the next fifteen minutes so that she could sit quietly and think about Helen.

The mental telepathy wouldn't work unless she was alone. She had to be able to close her eyes and concentrate, to shut out every distraction.

She couldn't ask Gretchen to leave, without telling her why. But she couldn't say why she wanted to be alone at five o'clock, either. Gretchen was probably still a little angry about finding Willow and Helen together at McDonald's. It would only hurt her feelings more to learn that Willow and Helen had a secret pact to think of each other every day at the same time.

"Well, do you or not?" Gretchen asked.

Willow blinked. "Do I what?"

Gretchen scowled at her. "Do you want to go over to my

65

house and do the new aerobics video my mom got?"

"Oh. No, not right now. But you go ahead."

"What's wrong with you?"

"Nothing's wrong."

"You haven't heard a word I've said."

"I'm just tired. That's why I don't want to do the aerobics video. I think I'll go take a nap."

Gretchen nodded, clearly unconvinced. Willow sneaked another look at her watch—4:55.

"I can't believe this," Gretchen said. "You want me to leave, don't you?"

"No. That is, I don't *want* you to leave, I just . . ."

"I don't think you're tired at all," Gretchen said. "And you don't want to take a nap, either. I don't know what you want to do, but I think it has something to do with that Helen. Am I right?"

Willow hesitated. She couldn't lie to Gretchen again. Gretchen was her best friend.

"Well. . . . ."

"I thought so," Gretchen said. "What is it with you and her? You probably won't ever see her again but you act like she's the most important person in your whole life. What's so great about her, anyway?"

"Nothing."

"Nothing? Ha! Ever since you met her, you've been different. You walk around zombie-eyed, staring into space. Last night, you dashed out of McDonald's after her with your face lit up as if you had just won the lottery."

"I had to tell her something."

"It must have been pretty important."

Willow knew Gretchen was curious. She wanted Willow to tell her what it was that was so important. But Willow couldn't tell Gretchen. Not now. There wasn't time to tell her now. It was almost five o'clock.

The mantle clock in the living room started to strike. Bong . . . Bong . . .

"I'll explain it all to you later," Willow said. "Right now I have to be alone."

She ran out of the kitchen and up the stairs, once again leaving Gretchen to stare after her.

"I'll call you tonight," Willow yelled, as she hurried into her own room.

"Don't bother. Believe me, I'll be much too tired to talk to you." The front door slammed behind Gretchen as Willow sank down on her bed.

She took two deep breaths and pushed everything else out of her mind.

I'm thinking only of you, Helen, she thought. I send my thoughts to you. I am lying on my bed. Sarah is worse today, and I made Gretchen angry because I wanted to be alone at five o'clock. Do you hear me? Are you receiving my thoughts?

Willow lay still. She stared so hard at the ceiling that her eyes felt like cotton balls.

She spoke out loud. "I'm waiting to receive your thoughts, Helen. Are you thinking of me?"

No answer. She closed her eyes and repeated the message. She waited. She heard some children playing tag. She heard Jericho bark. She covered her ears, to blot out the noise. How could she receive a message from Helen if she was thinking about Mrs. Clauson's dog?

She tried to concentrate, her thoughts focused only on Helen.

Helen . . . Helen . . . Helen . . .

Willow waited for fifteen minutes. Nothing happened. No vision of Helen popped into her mind. No message came magically across the continent. If Helen was sending thoughts to Willow, Willow was not receiving them.

She rode her bike to Gretchen's house and knocked on the door. There was no answer, so she knocked again. Finally Ryan opened the door.

"Gretchen says to tell you she isn't home," Ryan said.

"Tell her I came to explain."

"Explain what?"

"Just tell her. She'll know what I mean."

Moments later, Willow and Gretchen sat crosslegged on Gretchen's bed and Willow began. "First, you have to swear you won't tell anyone else what I'm going to tell you."

Gretchen's eyes grew round. "Are you in some kind of trouble?" she asked.

"Not trouble, exactly. Just a puzzle. It started on my birthday, when I almost drowned."

Willow went through everything that had happened, careful to include all the details so that Gretchen would understand why this was so important.

When she finished, she waited for Gretchen to respond. Gretchen was silent, her fingers picking at the nubs in the bedspread.

"Well?" Willow said.

"Are you saying you believe in reincarnation?" Gretchen whispered the question, as if she feared someone's ear might be pressed to the keyhole.

Willow nodded. "I saw myself in another life. I've met the girl who used to be my sister."

Gretchen looked as horrified as if Willow had announced plans to bomb an orphanage. "I think you should forget all of this," she said. "Pretend it never happened. Never try mental telepathy with Helen again. Don't write to her or call her, either."

"I don't want to forget it," Willow said. "I want to understand it. I want to know more about my past life."

"No!" Gretchen held up her hand and spoke with such intensity that Willow, startled, leaned away from her. "The things you're talking about are evil," Gretchen said.

"Evil! Why are they evil? You always talk about eternal life as if it's the most wonderful thing possible. Why is it suddenly evil?"

"Eternal life is what happens when you turn over your soul to Jesus. That isn't the same thing as reincarnation."

"Kalos and Tiy may have lived before Jesus," Willow said. "What were they supposed to do with their souls? Or has eternal life only been around for the last two thousand years?"

"I think The Devil has put bad ideas into your head," Gretchen said.

Willow stood up. "I shouldn't have told you," she said. "I knew you wouldn't understand. That's why I didn't say anything sooner."

"Come with me to talk to Pastor Farriday," Gretchen said. "He can tell you what to do. He can pray for The Devil's ideas to leave your mind."

"No, thanks."

"Then I'll go by myself and ask him to help you."

"You can't! You promised you wouldn't tell anyone."

"That was before I knew you were in serious trouble."

"I'm not in trouble. You talk like I got caught shoplifting or something."

"Shoplifting I could handle. I can't take on The Devil. Pastor Farriday says . . ."

"Did it ever occur to you to think for yourself," Willow said, "instead of always parroting your pastor?"

"I only want to help you," Gretchen said.

"It doesn't help to be told my ideas come from The Devil. And if you breathe one word of this to anyone, including Pastor Farriday, I swear I'll never speak to you again."

Gretchen looked down at her hands. "I have to do what's right," she said.

"What's right is to keep your promises."

Willow stormed out of Gretchen's room, trying not to cry.

10

DEAR HELEN:

I've tried seven times. Every day, at exactly five o'clock, I sit alone and think about you. I send my thoughts to you and I try to hear any message you are sending me.

Nothing happens. Nothing.

Are you doing it? Are you thinking of me at five o'clock every day, like we agreed?

Write and let me know because if you aren't going to do it, I'll quit, too.

The doctors have decided Sarah's best bet is to have a bone marrow transplant. The trouble is, it isn't easy to find a donor who matches. My whole family was tested. Not fun. I came the closest but I still wasn't a perfect match.

Yesterday the doctor registered Sarah with the National

Bone Marrow Program. It's in Minnesota. He says it's possible to do a transplant with tissue from a nonrelative if a donor can be found.

I wish you were here so we could talk. I feel all mixed up. Right now, my parents can't think of anything except Sarah. When I'm at the hospital, I can't think of anything else, either, but I don't stay at the hospital all the time. I get too antsy.

It's gone on such a long time. Once yesterday I caught myself wishing she would just die and get it over with. Then I felt like the lowest, scummiest worm in the world, for thinking such a thing.

I don't want her to die. I want her to live. I want her to get well and go to school and borrow my sweaters, like she always used to do.

The worst part is not knowing what's going to happen.

My parents are pretty freaked out. They try to act cheerful but they're scared. I can tell. Dad fidgets a lot and bites his nails, and Mom has an odd, vague look in her eyes, as if she had a nightmare too horrible to talk about. They never laugh.

When you're scared all the time, it's hard to laugh. I think that's what I miss most right now; nobody in our family laughs anymore.

This letter is depressing. Sorry about that. I guess I needed to dump on somebody. I used to be able to tell Gretchen my problems but we aren't getting along so hot.

Have you found out anything about ancient Egypt? I haven't had a chance to go to the library because I spend so much time with Sarah. I did have one neat thing happen, *though. Last night, when I took Muttsie outside for his walk, there were hundreds of stars, like twinkling polka dots on a black blanket.*

Then I saw the moon and I remembered that Kalos saw the moon, too, on her way to the temple, and it gave me the funniest feeling. There I was, looking at the very same moon and stars that I had looked at centuries ago, when I was someone else.

Somehow, it made me feel peaceful to know that the moon has been there for thousands of years. It was there in the lifetime of Kalos, and it's here for my lifetime now, and it was here for all of the years in between. The same stars will probably still be twinkling a thousand years from now.

Thinking about that made my problems less important. Even Sarah's illness doesn't seem so awful when I look at the moon and the stars.

Am I making any sense?

School starts Monday. I'm glad to think about something besides hospitals and bone marrow. But I feel guilty for being glad.

I've decided to tell Sarah about Kalos and Tiy and you. Maybe she wouldn't be so scared if she knew that this one life isn't all she gets. Who knows? Maybe she and I will be sisters again some time, or at least friends. If you and I found each other after all those centuries, maybe Sarah and I will find each other in another life, too.

I'm not scared of dying like I used to be—not for Sarah and not for myself. I still want to live as long as I can, though. No matter how many other lives I might have ahead of me, I don't want to hurry through this one. There are too many things I want to do. Like learn to water ski and graduate from college and (maybe, some day) get married.

I'm going to tell Sarah how I saw Grandma and Grandpa when I was drowning. Maybe all of this would be easier for her if she knew she was going to be with them.

I would have told her sooner except every time I started to tell her I thought, what if I'm wrong? What if all of this is just my imagination? Gretchen thinks it's sinful to think I lived before. What if she's right?

Please write back soon and tell me if the mental telepathy is working for you. I'll keep trying at five o'clock every day, until I hear from you.

Love, your sister (long ago),
Willow

P.S. Be sure to send me a picture.

11

WILLOW TOOK one bite of her grilled cheese sandwich and shoved the plate aside.

She had to do something to help Sarah. Anything! But what could she do? If the doctors and nurses and technicians couldn't help Sarah, what was a thirteen-year-old girl supposed to do?

She wished she had someone to talk to. Her parents were hardly ever home and when they were home, they were too strung out to discuss anything.

Always before, Willow could count on Gretchen to listen and sympathize and give advice. Now she couldn't call Gretchen. They had not spoken since their argument. Willow missed Gretchen terribly but she still thought Gretchen was wrong.

Willow wished her grandparents were still alive. Grandma

and Grandpa always had time to listen to her problems. Willow remembered how, when she was drowning, she felt that they were waiting for her.

She closed her eyes, pictured her grandmother in her mind and whispered, "What should I do, Grandma? How can I help Sarah?"

There was no answer. Willow opened her eyes, feeling foolish. I'm going bonkers, she thought. First I decide I've lived before and now I'm trying to talk to the dead.

She went to her room and got out her notebook. She would write to Helen one more time, even though Helen had not answered the previous letters.

As she opened the notebook, a small white card fluttered to the floor. Willow picked it up. It was the card that Mrs. Evans, the speaker at the library, had given her. Mrs. Evans had said to call her if Willow ever needed help.

The card said Mrs. Evans was a psychotherapist at a mental health clinic. Did that mean she worked with crazy people? Did she think Willow was crazy?

Maybe I am, Willow thought. Maybe I should call.

Without giving herself time to change her mind, Willow dialed the number on the card.

"Come right over," Mrs. Evans told her.

Half an hour later, Willow sat in Mrs. Evans's office, pouring out the whole story of Sarah's illness. "I want so much to help her," Willow said, "and I feel helpless because I can't."

"Have you tried sending your healing thoughts to her?" Mrs. Evans asked.

"I'm not sure what you mean."

"When you are alone in a quiet place, close your eyes

and think of Sarah. Imagine yourself holding her hands. Picture your strength and energy flowing into her body."

"Once when I held Sarah's hand, I felt a current between us, almost like electricity."

"Love. You felt love. When it's strong enough, it has a physical energy. It's the one thing you can give your sister," Mrs. Evans said, "and love is the most potent healing force there is."

"If that's true, shouldn't I go and really hold her hands, like I did before, rather than just imagining it?"

"Of course. Be with her whenever you can. But if you can't be there in person, visualization can still help. You may have heard about athletes who prepare for a race or a game by imagining exactly what they will do. A runner might visualize herself being the first to cross the finish line."

"Yes. I've heard of that."

"This is the same thing. The mind tells the body what to do and the body responds." Mrs. Evans smiled at her. "Tell me how you came to be interested in past-life regression," she said.

Willow explained how she nearly drowned, and about the visions and the dream, and how she found Helen. She also told about her problems with Gretchen. When she finished, she asked, "Do you think I lived before, as Kalos?"

"It doesn't matter what I think," Mrs. Evans said. "As long as you believe it, it is true for you. And your friend, Gretchen. She believes certain things, too."

"Yes."

"Then for her those things are true, whether you think so or not. Don't try to change her mind; don't say that her beliefs aren't true. Truth has nothing to do with belief."

"You're saying we can disagree and still be friends?"

"Of course. How boring life would be if we all thought alike."

"The trouble is," Willow said slowly, "Gretchen thinks *her* beliefs are right and anything else is wrong. She accepts what she is told without questioning it."

Mrs. Evans nodded sympathetically. "Many people prefer to do that. You are learning that each person has his own truth; Gretchen doesn't know that yet."

"She sure doesn't."

"It may be harder for Gretchen to accept new ideas than it is for you, because of her upbringing. It isn't easy to challenge the things you're taught as a child."

"My parents *are* more flexible than Gretchen's are," Willow admitted. "So what should I do—pretend to agree with her?"

Mrs. Evans shook her head, no. "You can value Gretchen just as she is, even if you don't accept all her views. You're friends, not clones. Accept her as she is; don't try to change her. Ask her to accept you."

"I'm not so sure she will do that," Willow said.

"Ask her. What do you have to lose by asking? And tell her you've missed her."

"OK," Willow said. "I'll try it. And I'll send my love and energy to Sarah."

"Good. I'll send my healing thoughts to Sarah, too. Let me know how she gets along."

Willow promised that she would. As soon as she got home, she called Gretchen.

"I miss you," she said. "I'm sorry if I hurt your feelings."

"Believe me, I miss you, too," Gretchen said.

"Can you come over? I want to talk to you."

"Be there in half an hour."

While she waited, Willow decided to read the Personals. Maybe there would be a good letter, something she and Gretchen could laugh about, the way they used to.

She turned to the classified section and skimmed the page.

Jericho. The name caught her attention and Willow looked more closely. It was under Lost and Found:

LOST: Cocker spaniel. Beloved family pet. Wearing red collar with the name Jericho on it. Generous reward.

There was also a telephone number.

Willow read the notice twice. Jericho wasn't a common name for a dog. And the dog that Mrs. Clauson took out of her car was definitely a cocker spaniel.

Could Mrs. Clauson have found two lost dogs in such a short period of time? First the poodle and now the cocker? It seemed like too much of a coincidence.

Willow went outside and looked to see if Jericho was in the yard next door. He was.

"Here, Jericho," she said. She put her fingers through the fence. "Good Jericho. Come, boy."

The dog galloped toward her, wagging his tail.

Just then, Mrs. Clauson came out on her porch. "Is there something you want, Willow?" she asked.

"I was just going to pet the dog."

"It's time for his dinner," Mrs. Clauson said. "Come, Jericho."

The dog stopped. He looked at Mrs. Clauson and then at Willow.

"Jericho!" Mrs. Clauson snapped. "Come here."

Jericho trotted to the door and Mrs. Clauson put him inside. But not before Willow saw that he wore a red collar.

"How long will Jericho be staying with you?" she asked.

"His owners should be back any day." Mrs. Clauson frowned at her. "Why do you ask?"

"No reason," Willow said. "I just wondered."

Was it possible that Jericho wasn't being boarded? Was he, perhaps, *stolen*?

She didn't like the way Mrs. Clauson looked at her. Had her suspicions been obvious? She turned and hurried back to her own house. When she was safely inside, she sat on the floor, close to Muttsie. She nuzzled her face in his fur, inhaling his warm doggie smell.

When Gretchen arrived, Willow showed her the Lost ad and told her about the dog next door. "I think she takes someone's dog and keeps it until a reward is offered. Then she pretends she found the dog. After she returns it and collects the money, she steals somebody else's dog."

"I can't believe anyone would do that," Gretchen said. "How could she be sure the dog's owner would pay a reward? Some people wouldn't even bother to advertise. Then she'd be stuck with a dog she doesn't want. What would she do, try to sneak it back home again?"

Willow shrugged. "I don't know," she said.

"There's no way she could be certain, before she took a dog, that its owners would be willing to pay a reward."

"You're right," Willow said. "It's probably just a coincidence that she happens to be taking care of a cocker spaniel named Jericho who's wearing a red collar." She looked at the Lost ad again. "Unless . . ." she said. "Unless there's another way to get money. If the owner doesn't offer a reward, maybe Mrs. Clauson sells the dog somewhere else."

Gretchen looked dubious. "Where?"

"I've read about cosmetics companies that use animals to test products like shampoo and mascara."

Gretchen shuddered. "But they're *pets*," she said. "I can't believe she would sell someone's pet. Would she?"

Willow didn't answer. She looked at Muttsie. She thought about the way Jericho's tail had thumped on the car seat when she spoke kindly to him. She remembered how Mrs. Clauson sounded when she was negotiating for a larger reward for the poodle. Willow picked up the newspaper and walked to the telephone.

"What are you going to do?" Gretchen asked.

"Call the people and tell them that I think my neighbor might have their dog."

"What if they come here and it isn't their dog? Mrs. Clauson will be furious."

"I know. But I still think I should call."

"So do I."

Willow dialed the number. The line was busy. She waited a few minutes and dialed again. Still busy.

Finally, on the third try, it rang. Someone answered almost immediately.

"Hello," Willow said. "I saw your ad in the paper about a lost dog and I . . ."

"We already found our dog."

"You did?"

"Yes, just a few minutes ago. But thanks for calling, anyway. Good-bye."

Willow hung up. "They already found him. I guess I really jumped to the wrong conclusion that time. I would have sworn that . . ."

"Shhh." Gretchen stood beside the window, peering out. "She's putting Jericho in the car."

Willow walked to the window and stood on the other side. Both girls watched as Mrs. Clauson opened her car door and urged Jericho to hop inside. Then she got in the driver's side, started the engine, and drove away.

"Where do you suppose she's taking him?" Gretchen asked. "Less than an hour ago, she told you his owners weren't back yet, so she can't be taking him home. Besides, they would probably come here, to get him."

"She's taking him to meet his owner," Willow said slowly. "And collect the reward. When she realized I was suspicious, she called the owner and arranged to return Jericho right away."

"That's why the line was busy when you called."

"Right."

"But why would she wait until you acted suspicious before she called? I can't believe she would keep him longer than necessary."

"Maybe . . ." Willow thought about the conversation she'd overheard. "Maybe she waits until the owners are so worried that they'll agree to a bigger reward. Probably the longer the dog is missing, the more frantic the owners get."

"That's terrible," Gretchen said. "Mrs. Clauson doesn't seem that mean. And we can't prove it."

"We can't prove it yet. But I'm going to start keeping track of what kinds of dogs Mrs. Clauson has, and when she has them."

"Good idea."

"And we'll read the Lost ads every day, to see if any of them match the dogs Mrs. Clauson has."

"Right."

"If she really is stealing the dogs in order to collect the reward money," Willow said, "we'll be able to prove it eventually."

"Let's call Jericho's owner again tomorrow. Ask who returned him."

"I'd bet two weeks' allowance," Willow said, "that it's Mrs. Clauson."

12

DEAR HELEN:

I'm going to be hypnotized. Not plain old hypnotized. I'm going to be hypnotized by a professional hypnotherapist for the purpose of being regressed to a previous life.

Can you believe it? I can't, either.

Here's what happened. I called Mrs. Evans to tell her how Sarah is. Mrs. Evans said she is conducting a workshop in Past-Life Regression and she offered to let me come. For free! She said she knew I was going through a hard time right now and she thought I might like something else to think about. Would I ever!

The workshop will be a guided visualization, where a group of people gets hypnotized at the same time and each one regresses to his or her own past lives. I can hardly wait!

There's only one catch. Mrs. Evans says I must have permission from my parents and I haven't told them anything about Kalos yet. Cross your fingers that they'll let me go.

If they do, I'll write and tell you about it. Maybe I'll get to see Kalos again. And Tiy.

Love,
Willow

P.S. Why don't you write? Should I keep thinking about you at five o'clock or not?
P.P.S. I think my next-door neighbor is a dognapper!

13

WOULD SHE see herself as Kalos again tonight? Would she see Helen as Tiy? As Willow rode the bus to the workshop, she hoped Mrs. Evans would help her go back to that other life, to learn more about the time when she lived in a mud house near the Nile River and worshiped the sun god, Amun-Ra.

Willow had not yet told her parents about Kalos or even about her vision of Grandma and Grandpa. They knew she'd met Helen but they had no idea that Helen used to be Tiy.

It wasn't that Willow wanted to keep her experiences secret. Mr. and Mrs. Paige had always encouraged Willow and Sarah to explore new ideas, so she knew she could tell them about the visions and the dream and about sending her love to Sarah through visualization. She was sure they would understand her curiosity and be interested in her experiences.

But she couldn't tell them now. Her parents were so concerned about Sarah that they hardly listened to anything Willow said these days. And she didn't want to discuss something so important until she had their full attention. After Sarah got well, she would tell them everything.

At breakfast that morning, she gave her father Mrs. Evans's business card and said, "This woman is giving a workshop tonight and I'd like to go, if it's OK with you. I'd need a ride home afterwards."

Mr. Paige read the card. "Where did you get this?" he asked. "Do you know her?"

"I heard her give a speech one Saturday at the Bellefield Library."

"What's the workshop about?"

Before Willow could answer, her mother came into the kitchen and said, "The hospital just called. They've put Sarah on oxygen."

"I'll try to get away from work early," Mr. Paige said. He looked at Willow. "What time should I pick you up tonight?"

"Ten o'clock. The address is on the card."

Mr. Paige nodded and put the business card in his pocket. Nothing more was said about the workshop.

At seven o'clock that night, Willow sat in Mrs. Evans's office, along with the ten other people in the workshop, and listened to Mrs. Evans talk about reincarnation.

"There are several theories," she said. "My favorite is that before we are born, we are in a planning room, where we plan who we will be and who we will be with. At birth, we come through a tunnel to the Earth Plane. When we die, we go back through the tunnel to a debriefing room and eventually, we return to planning again and the whole process is repeated."

Willow wondered if that was possible. Do we have some choice about when we are born and who we have for parents or brothers or sisters?

If that's true, Willow thought, and we really can choose who we will be with, people who love each other might be able to be together again in more than one lifetime.

Someone said, "That's why some people call each other soul mates. They believe they find each other in life after life."

"It's one theory," Mrs. Evans said. "There are others and there's no way to prove any of them." She smiled. "Not in this life, anyway."

After some more discussion about reincarnation, Mrs. Evans instructed everyone to lie down on the floor. It was time for Willow and the others to try to see a past life.

Willow's head rested comfortably on a pillow. She closed her eyes and listened.

"Nothing negative can happen in this workshop," Mrs. Evans said. "Only positive feelings will result from what we do."

Willow was glad to hear that.

"Take deep breaths," Mrs. Evans said. "Relax your feet. Breathe deeply and relax your legs."

Willow took deep breaths and followed instructions.

"Imagine a big jar," Mrs. Evans said. "Put all your worries into the jar."

Willow pictured herself putting Sarah's leukemia in a jar. Then she put Gretchen's talk of The Devil in the jar. Next she put in her suspicions about Mrs. Clauson and, for good measure, she added her concern about why she hadn't heard from Helen.

"Now put a lid on that jar," Mrs. Evans said. "Screw it on tightly. None of your worries and cares can get out until you unscrew the lid."

Mrs. Evans's voice grew softer. "Imagine a hole in the top of your head," she said. "You can see out through the hole, out into the vast beyond. See yourself lift out through the hole. You float upward and enter a tunnel. You move through the tunnel. On the other side is a safe place . . . your favorite place. As you approach this favorite place, you are surrounded by white light. It is a bright, white light which protects you and keeps all harm from you."

Willow felt the white light surround her. It encased her like a glowing shield. Safe and relaxed, she slipped easily out the hole in her head and floated up through the tunnel.

When she emerged from the tunnel at the other end, she was in a huge room with high ceilings and fancy carved woodwork. Her long green gown had lace trim on the sleeves and throat. Massive oil paintings hung on the walls and marble statues stood on the floral carpet. Through an archway, she saw a group of men, all wearing white wigs and buckled shoes.

"Continue backwards in time," Mrs. Evans said. "Leave the place you see now and journey farther, back to another time."

Willow felt herself float away from the room with the paintings. It was like watching herself in a movie. The film gradually faded away from one scene and into the next one.

This time, she was on horseback. It was a white horse,

wearing lavish red and gold trappings. Willow wore red tights, high boots, and a short white uniform with long red sleeves. A dagger hung from her belt. She realized she was seeing herself as a man. She was in a procession with many other riders, climbing a rocky path up a steep hillside.

While she saw these scenes in her mind, Willow was still aware that she was on the floor in Mrs. Evans's office. She heard the person next to her clear his throat and she heard the coffee pot gurgle. It was as if she were in two places at the same time.

"Leave this scene now," Mrs. Evans said. "Let it disappear as you continue backwards in time. Go farther this time. Go as far back as you can and look for someone you recognize."

As the horseback procession faded, Willow felt buoyant, as if she were a puff of cotton candy, floating through the sky. Gradually, another scene came into focus. Willow saw palm trees against a cloudless sky. She smiled as she recognized Kalos.

Kalos and Tiy sat on the ground, playing a game. There was a board between them, and many small carved pieces of wood. Some of the wooden pieces had dog heads and some had jackal heads.

"If you think you see yourself as you were in another lifetime," Mrs. Evans said, "step back through time and greet that other self. Hug him or her."

Willow saw herself approach Kalos and hug her. Kalos laughed and hugged her back.

"Ask that person if he or she has any message for you," Mrs. Evans said.

Willow didn't ask right away. Instead, she hugged Tiy.

Although Tiy seemed surprised, she let Willow hug her.

A small girl stood watching them. The girl smiled shyly at Willow and held out her arms to be hugged, too. Willow looked questioningly at Kalos.

Kalos smiled. "Huzein," she said, pointing at the child.

Willow took a step toward the girl. Something about her was familiar, though Willow was sure she'd never seen the child before.

As Willow approached the little girl, she heard Mrs. Evans say, "You're going to come back now. Back through the tunnel. Back to the present."

Willow wasn't ready to leave. She wanted to find out who the little girl was and she had not yet asked Kalos about a message.

"You're drifting up," Mrs. Evans said. "Back through time. Back to the tunnel."

Although she was reluctant to leave Kalos and Tiy so soon, Willow decided to follow instructions.

Kalos, Tiy, and the little girl faded away.

Willow entered the tunnel again and slid easily back into her own body.

"Rest a few moments now," Mrs. Evans said. "Breathe deeply. Sleep, if you want to. You are safe. Only good things will happen here tonight."

Willow took deep breaths. She felt the white light around her like a transparent slipcover. She relaxed completely. Her breath came slowly. She fell soundly asleep and began to dream.

In the dream, it was early on a Sunday morning. Willow decided to go out, to buy fresh rolls for breakfast.

As she walked away from her house she saw a festive, outdoor carnival where people sold handmade crafts. Pottery jugs, painted rich blues and golds, bloomed in the green grass. Papier-mâché dragons lounged on red picnic blankets. The aroma of cinnamon hung in the air.

Everywhere she looked, colorful flags flew from long poles and bright banners waved in the breeze. Warm sunshine filtered through the leaves of large chestnut trees. Underfoot, smooth cobblestone streets curved gracefully in all directions, inviting her to explore them. She was astonished that such a place existed so close to her home. Why had she never discovered it?

Music played in the distance—happy music, the kind that a circus calliope might play. Willow strolled down one of the streets. Everyone smiled at her. Clearly, all of the people at the carnival were there because they wanted to be there and not because they needed to sell their wares to earn money. She had never seen any place like this, had never felt this kind of community joy.

She stopped at a wooden booth where a glassblower in a purple cap was making glass unicorns.

"How long will the carnival be here?" Willow asked.

"Why, it's always here," the glassblower said. "It's open, free of charge, to anyone who chooses to come."

"Always?" Willow said. "Every day?"

"Every day. Forever."

Willow thanked him and started to walk on.

Forever!

She stopped. She had to share this discovery. She would bring Sarah here; she would show Sarah this splendid place.

She would tell Sarah that, any time she wanted to, she could visit the carnival.

She turned and hurried down the cobblestone street, going back to get Sarah.

When she passed a booth that sold prancing clay ponies, she heard Mrs. Evans say, "You're going to come back now. Wake up. Come back to the present. Come back to this room."

As Willow listened to Mrs. Evans, the cobblestone streets faded away and she began to wake up.

"You feel rested," Mrs. Evans said. "You feel relaxed and energized. As you return to this room, the white light still surrounds you. It is all around you, keeping you safe. When you wake up, you will feel happy. When I count to five, you'll be completely awake. One . . . two . . . three . . . the light is around you . . . four . . . ready, now . . . five."

Willow opened her eyes. No one spoke. She wondered if the others felt as good as she felt. She had expected the workshop to be interesting but she had not anticipated anything like what she had experienced.

She was elated, especially by the carnival. The carnival had been fantastic and the delight she felt while she was there stayed with her when she was back in the room with Mrs. Evans and the others.

Best of all, since the carnival was only in her mind, she could go there any time she wanted to, simply by thinking of it. The glassblower was right. The carnival was always there. It would be there forever.

After a few moments, Mrs. Evans said, "Does anyone want to share what they saw?"

Several people told of seeing themselves in other lifetimes

but Willow did not speak. She wanted time alone, to examine her feelings. She needed to think about the little girl with Kalos. She wanted to write down everything about the carnival, to be sure she would never forget it.

Tomorrow, she would tell Sarah about it. She was sorry she ran out of time in her dream before she could get Sarah and take her to the carnival but at least she could describe it to Sarah.

There was just one thing that bothered her.

People stood up, gathered their coats, and began to leave.

Willow approached Mrs. Evans. "After I came back through the tunnel, I saw myself at a carnival," she said. "A wonderful carnival. Only it was *me* there. Me, Willow, not some other me who lived long ago."

"That's all right," Mrs. Evans said. "You were probably dreaming."

"I don't understand," Willow said. "Was it just a regular dream, like I might have at home? Or was I seeing myself in another life even though I still looked the same?"

"How do you feel, Willow?" Mrs. Evans asked.

"Great. The carnival was a happy place."

"Then it doesn't really matter, does it, whether you were dreaming or seeing yourself in another lifetime? What matters is how you feel now and if you feel wonderful, it was a good experience."

Willow nodded. "I like the white light," she said.

"Ah. So you are one of us."

"One of you?"

"Not everyone feels the light. When I explain it, many people look blank. They have no idea what I mean."

94

"I felt it," Willow said. "I still feel it. It's all around me. It's . . ." She searched for words to explain what she felt.

"It is all goodness and love and kindness."

"Yes." Willow smiled at her. "I know." She *did* know. Even before it was put into words, she knew. She also knew that, whenever she wanted to, she could surround herself with the white light.

It was around her as she left the room. Although the light was invisible, she felt luminous. It radiated from her, and floated up to the stars.

Her father was waiting for her. As she climbed in the car, she saw the weariness in his eyes and she willed the white light to flow around him, too. She wanted to share her joy.

"The workshop was wonderful," she said. "When I get home, I'm going to write everything down. I want to remember the details when I tell Sarah about it tomorrow."

Mr. Paige looked down at his hands. "Sarah," he said, "has slipped into a coma."

14

"I'M GOING back to the hospital," Mr. Paige said. "Do you want to go there, too? If not, I can either drop you at Gretchen's or I can take you home."

"Is Mom still at the hospital?"

"Yes."

"I'll go with you. What does the coma mean?"

"It isn't good. We had hoped to have a donor before this."

Willow closed her eyes and tried to hang on to the feeling of peace and joy that she'd had when the workshop ended. Instead, she felt like the jar containing all of her worries had just been smashed with a hammer.

When they got to the hospital, Willow asked her parents if they had eaten any dinner.

"No. We didn't want to leave Sarah by herself—and neither of us felt like eating alone."

"I'll stay with Sarah," Willow said. "You go get a sandwich."

Mrs. Paige put her arm around Willow's shoulder and hugged her.

As soon as her parents left, Willow stood beside Sarah's bed. Sarah's breathing was so shallow that Willow had to watch closely to be sure she was breathing at all.

She took one of Sarah's hands in both of hers and closed her eyes. She thought about the white light; immediately, she felt it around her. The calmness returned.

She visualized the light going from her hand to Sarah's. It crept under the blanket and encircled Sarah's body.

She whispered, "I give you my energy, Sarah, and my strength. Love is flowing from my body into yours. You are now protected by the white light. It surrounds you and it will keep you safe."

Willow didn't wonder what to say or how to say it. The words came from somewhere deep within her; all she had to do was let them out.

"My love and my strength are pouring into you," she continued, her voice getting louder. "The white light will help you. Think about it. Feel it around you."

Sarah stirred slightly.

Encouraged, Willow kept talking. "I give you my energy. I give you my love. It will heal you. The white light is all around you. Love will heal . . ."

"What are you doing?"

The man's harsh voice was directly behind Willow. She jumped and dropped Sarah's hand. Spinning around, she looked to see who was in the room.

It was Sarah's doctor.

"Hello, Dr. Rogers," she said.

Dr. Rogers squinted at her. "I heard what you said to Sarah." He sounded upset.

Willow said nothing.

Dr. Rogers moved toward Sarah's bed, lifted her wrist, and took her pulse. He made a note on Sarah's chart.

"I thought you were here in the mornings," Willow said.

"I'm on call tonight and I came in for another patient. Since I'm here anyway, I decided to check Sarah, too."

"Oh."

She wished Dr. Rogers would leave. She wanted more time alone with Sarah before her parents returned.

He didn't seem in any hurry. He stood there looking at Willow, as if trying to decide what else to say to her. Finally he said, "I'd like to talk to you for a moment. In the hall."

Willow nodded and followed him.

When they were in the hall outside Sarah's room, Dr. Rogers said, "I think I should warn you not to give your sister any false hope for a cure. It's all right to pray with her but be careful what you say. Just because she's not conscious doesn't mean she can't hear you. I believe a patient in a coma hears everything that's said in their presence."

"I wanted her to hear me," Willow said. "I want to help her get well."

"Healing is my job." He said it emphatically, accenting the word *my*.

Willow bit her bottom lip. He acted like she'd done something harmful, something that would make Sarah worse. She wanted to justify her motives, to make it clear that she loved Sarah and was only trying to help her.

"I learned about the white light," she said, "and I want Sarah to know about it, too. It's wonderful! It's all goodness and . . ."

"White light?" He frowned. "Do your parents know you do this when you're alone with your sister?"

"No. I never did it before." She couldn't tell if Dr. Rogers believed her or not. Why was he making her feel so guilty when all she wanted to do was help?

"I suggest that your first time also be your last. Leave the science of healing to the physicians. We're trained for it. You aren't, no matter how much faith you have."

It was all Willow could do not to point out that the doctors, despite all their training, weren't doing Sarah much good.

Willow fought back her tears as Dr. Rogers walked away. Then she went back in Sarah's room. She looked at Sarah. She blinked and looked again.

Sarah's eyes were open!

Willow leaned over the bed. "Are you awake? Can you hear me?"

"Hi," Sarah said. Her voice was feeble but it sounded glorious to Willow.

"Do you need anything? A drink of water?"

"Just talk to me. I heard you talking to me before. I feel better when you talk to me."

"Listen carefully," Willow said. "I have something important to tell you. Things have happened to me. I've learned something that you need to know."

Sarah looked puzzled but she nodded her head slightly, to tell Willow to continue.

"It started on my birthday," Willow began. "It started when I almost drowned." She told Sarah everything. She described the visions and the dream about Kalos and Amun-Ra. She told Sarah about Helen and about Mrs. Evans. She told her about the white light and the carnival and how she wasn't afraid of death anymore.

"No matter what happens," Willow said, "it isn't the end. If you don't live through all this, you'll go to be with Grandma and Grandpa. I still hope you'll live—I want you to get well and come home and be my sister for years and years—but if you don't, at least we know it isn't the end of everything. You'll go someplace good and be with people you love. And we'll be together again, some day, somewhere."

Sarah smiled at Willow. "I'm a perennial," she said. "Like the peonies."

"That's right. Sarah Peony."

"I want to feel the white light again," Sarah said.

"You felt it?"

"Yes. Tell me about it again."

Willow hesitated, remembering Dr. Rogers's warning to leave the healing to the doctors. Then she saw the look in Sarah's eyes. Hope. For the first time in many days, Sarah looked hopeful.

I didn't need Pete Wellington, after all, Willow thought. I've given Sarah something to look forward to.

She grasped Sarah's hand and looked directly into Sarah's eyes. "We are surrounded by a white light," she said. "It's around me and it's around you. It keeps us safe."

There it was again—the feeling of electric-like current connecting her to Sarah. Sarah must have felt it, too, because she smiled and whispered, "I love you, Willow Sweet Pea."

"I love you, too. And love will help to heal you. It's going into you now, from my hand to yours."

Willow talked until her parents returned. When she heard them coming, she stopped talking and turned around. Dr. Rogers was with them.

"Sarah's awake," Willow said. "She's feeling better."

15

IT WAS five o'clock. Again. Still no letter from Helen. Still no evidence that Helen was trying to communicate.

Willow sat on her bed, with her knees drawn up. Muttsie was curled in a ball beside her; Willow absently scratched Muttsie behind the ears.

She felt like she'd been on an emotional roller coaster for weeks. She longed for an ordinary day, the kind she used to have before Sarah got sick.

She put her head on her knees and closed her eyes. She tried to think about Helen but other thoughts crowded into her mind. In particular, she remembered what had happened that day in her Social Studies class.

The students were giving oral reports and one boy, Jeff, gave his report on well-known people who use their fame for their own financial gain, at considerable cost to a gullible public. As his first example, he used sports stars who make beer commercials. For his second example, he used a movie actress who wrote a book claiming that she'd lived before.

"Thousands of people have wasted their money on this trash," Jeff said. "And on psychics and channelers and the other garbage she talks about in the book. She made up some far-out stories about how she lived hundreds of years ago in China and Africa. People believe them, just because she's a famous actress."

At the end of each speech, the class was supposed to ask questions. When Jeff finished, Willow raised her hand. "Why are you so sure," she said, "that the things in the book are not true?"

"Because she can't prove that she lived before."

"Can you prove that she didn't?"

Someone snickered and Jeff glared at Willow.

"I suppose," he said, "you believe in reincarnation. And in spirit channeling and . . ."

The teacher broke in. "Let's limit our discussion to questions and answers about the speech," he said and he called on someone else for a question. That would have been the end of the matter except that, as the students left the room after class, Jeff came up behind Willow and said loudly, "No doubt you were once the Queen of England."

Several kids laughed and the rest of the day they called her, "Queenie."

Willow had never had a lot of friends. She got along OK; she was accepted by her classmates and she wasn't lonely, but she always felt different somehow. Even with Gretchen, she had never completely belonged and lately her experiences had widened the gap.

Gretchen thought reincarnation was evil. Jeff and the others thought it was a hoax. What would Jeff think if he knew about Kalos?

She thought about Kalos and Tiy outside the temple. She remembered how she prayed to Amun-Ra and how thrilled she was when the sun's rays shone directly on the altar. The feeling she had when Tiy touched her hand was the same way she felt now about Sarah.

"I was Kalos," she whispered. "I know it! I was Kalos and Helen was Tiy." Tears welled up behind her closed eyelids. Send me a message, Helen, she pleaded silently. Send me your thoughts.

She sat quietly. Listening. Waiting.

I am thinking of you.

The phrase came out of nowhere. It was not spoken aloud, yet it seemed to echo in Willow's mind. Willow felt a tingling in her face.

She waited.

I think of you every day and wish the best for you and for your sister.

"I hear you," Willow whispered. "I know you're there."

She waited again. No more words came.

Willow raised her head and looked around. Her room looked exactly the same as it did last month. The dotted swiss curtains still hung at the window. Her bulletin board was still cluttered with notes and pictures. Her teddy bear collection still sat on top of the bookcase. Nothing was changed.

Nothing was changed, yet everything was different. Willow knew she had just experienced mental telepathy. She had communicated with another person, a person who was many miles away. And she knew this experience, like her experiences with the white light and the carnival and Kalos, had changed her.

She was not the same person today that she was when she woke up the morning of her birthday and prepared to go to Pinecone Lake with Gretchen. She was not even the same now as she was at five o'clock, just ten short minutes earlier. She looked the same, but inside she was different.

In the last few weeks, she had opened her mind to limitless possibilities. She wasn't sure where her new ideas and knowledge and feelings would lead her and she was nervous about exploring them. What would happen next?

Dr. Rogers disapproved of her efforts to help Sarah. Gretchen acted like she expected Willow to sink into hell at any moment. The kids at school scoffed and called her, "Queenie." Was it worth it?

When she was alone, her ideas seemed logical. Her dreams and visions seemed wonderful. And the white light. She felt it shining in her, through her, around her.

Was she going crazy? Or did the white light mean she had a special gift which enabled her to feel love and joy more deeply than most people?

"You're one of us," Mrs. Evans had said.

One of who? Weirdos who hallucinate?

And yet . . .

So far, her new ideas were exciting. The white light didn't make her feel weird; it made her feel special. She *had* helped Sarah; she was sure of it.

Now she had heard Helen's thoughts, from hundreds of miles away. She wondered if Helen was learning about Egypt. She hoped so, since Willow had not had time to go to the library.

The telephone rang. Willow wanted to ignore it but it might be one of her parents, calling from the hospital.

"Hello."

"It's me. Gretchen. Have you seen tonight's paper?"

"No."

"You won't believe this. There's a new ad for a lost dog and they're offering a two-hundred-dollar reward."

"What kind of dog is it?"

"It says, '*Lost: Female Welsh Corgi. Taken from family car. Two-hundred-dollar reward. No questions asked.*' Can you believe it? No questions asked. It's almost as if they know somebody took the dog in order to get a reward. Somebody like your sweet neighbor."

"I haven't seen Mrs. Clauson since the night she drove off with Jericho."

"Did you call Jericho's owners back? Did you find out who found their dog for them?"

"I called but they were no help. They didn't know the name of the person who returned Jericho and they didn't see her car. They said it was a gray-haired lady. Very sweet."

"Ha! Sweet like poison. Does she have a dog there now?"

"I don't know. I haven't done anything for two days except go to school and go to the hospital."

"Go look and call me back."

"I don't know what a Welsh Corgi looks like."

"I looked them up in my encyclopedia. They have short legs and pointed muzzles. They look kind of like a Dachshund, only they're brown and white."

Willow went outside and looked over the fence into Mrs. Clauson's backyard. There was no dog. She walked around to the front and strolled down the sidewalk, trying to see through Mrs. Clauson's living room windows. She saw no one.

She called Gretchen back and reported.

"Keep your eyes open," Gretchen advised. "Believe me, if she has this one, it would be the evidence we need."

"I'll try to watch but I'm not home much these days. The only reason you caught me at home now is that Mom sent me to get Sarah's tape player and some tapes. She thinks familiar music might be soothing."

"You sound stressed out."

"I am. My folks are, too."

"I put Sarah's name on the prayer chain at church."

"The what?"

"It's a group of people who agree to say prayers for anyone who's sick or in trouble. The first person prays and then calls the next one and they do the same. Each one is a link in the prayer chain."

"Oh." She wondered how people could pray for someone they didn't know. What would they say?

"You don't mind, do you?" Gretchen asked. "I know you aren't a Christian but I think prayers can help and . . ."

"I don't mind. Sarah needs all the help she can get. Thanks for putting her name in."

After they hung up, Willow thought about the prayer chain. In a way, those people were sending love, just like Willow did. Maybe when she put her hands on Sarah and tried to share the white light, she was doing the same thing that Gretchen's Christian friends tried to do with prayer. Maybe her beliefs and Gretchen's weren't so far apart, after all.

The telephone rang again. This time, it was Mrs. Paige. For the first time in months, there was enthusiasm in her voice.

"Dr. Rogers was just here," she said. "The Bone Marrow Program in Minnesota called him. They have a donor for Sarah."

Willow's heart began to race. "Who is it?" she asked.

"We aren't allowed to know who the donor is until a year after the transplant. All he could tell me is that it's a woman from another state."

People are good, Willow thought. A woman who doesn't even know Sarah is willing to do this for us.

"When is she coming?" Willow asked.

"She doesn't have to come. She'll donate the marrow in her own city and it will be sent here, in plasma."

"They *mail* it?"

"It's sent by air, in a cooler. It keeps a long time, at the right temperature. Dr. Rogers says it can even be frozen and kept several years."

"When will it get here?"

"I don't know yet. You don't need to come back with the tapes, though. Sarah's moving to a different room. She needs radiotherapy to help her immune system be ready to receive the donor marrow."

Her mother was in a hurry so Willow didn't ask any more questions. She didn't ask the one question that worried her most. How risky was this transplant? Was there a chance that Sarah wouldn't live through it?

16

WILLOW LOOKED at the return address: Scotland. What was Helen doing in Scotland? She ripped open the envelope.

Dear Willow,

I'm sorry I didn't write sooner but as you can see I am no longer in San Francisco. The day I got home, my dad told me he was being sent to Edinburgh for two years. I had one day to pack. It wasn't easy.

Anyway, I've been here ever since. We've seen the Royal Botanic Gardens and Holyrood Palace and some art museums. I'm getting educated, even though I haven't started school here yet.

Your letters were forwarded and got here today. I hope you haven't wasted too much time trying to receive thoughts from me. That first day, I rushed around getting packed and forgot all about our five o'clock deal. The second day, we were traveling.

After I got here, I discovered that five o'clock for you is now the middle of the night for me. So we can't try mental telepathy, after all. It would have been a fun experiment, if I had stayed in San Francisco.

I hope your sister is doing OK.

Your friend,
Helen

Willow read the letter again. There was not one word about Kalos and Tiy. No mention of that other lifetime. Helen obviously had not tried to learn about ancient Egypt. Either Helen had decided that she and Willow *weren't* sisters once, or else it wasn't important to her to know more.

Although Willow was disappointed, she understood why Helen might not be convinced of a past life. Helen had not seen herself as Tiy. She never dreamed about the temple and the great sun god, Amun-Ra.

Willow frowned. The day before at five o'clock she clearly heard: *I am thinking of you.*

If Helen *wasn't* thinking of her, why did she get that message? Who was it from?

She was sure she didn't imagine it. The words had been too distinct. Now that she thought of it, the rest of the message, *I wish the best for you and your sister*, wasn't phrased the way Willow would expect Helen to speak. It was too formal. Helen would have said, "I hope your sister is doing OK," just like she did in her letter.

Great, Willow thought. Now I'm hearing voices.

She decided not to answer Helen's letter. What was there to say? She still believed that she and Helen were sisters in a past life. But that life was over. This life is what concerned her now. This life, with her parents, and Gretchen, and school. This life—with Sarah scheduled for her bone marrow transplant tomorrow.

Willow went into the kitchen and poured a glass of apple juice. As she drank it, she looked out the window and all thoughts of Helen vanished.

There was a dog in Mrs. Clauson's yard. A small, brown dog that looked something like a Dachshund. After the way Mrs. Clauson glared at her when she found Willow calling Jericho, Willow didn't particularly want to go outside and try to get closer to the dog. But it fit Gretchen's description.

Willow put down her juice and called Gretchen.

"I think Mrs. Clauson might have the Welsh Corgi," she said. "I'm not sure if that's what kind it is. Can you come over? We can look at it through the binoculars."

Gretchen got there in record time. "Mom was just leaving to go to the dentist," she said, "so she gave me a ride over. I brought the encyclopedia and the Lost ad."

Gretchen examined the dog through the binoculars while Willow studied the picture of a Welsh Corgi in the book.

"That's it," Willow said.

"It sure is. Let's call."

Willow dialed the number. A woman answered.

"I'm calling about your dog," Willow said.

"Do you have her? Do you have Bonnie?"

"I'm not sure if it's your dog or not," Willow said. "It's a Welsh Corgi, though."

"Where was she? Where did you find her? Oh, I'm so relieved. I was sure someone stole her. She's never jumped out of the car before."

"Maybe she didn't jump this time, either," Willow said. "My neighbor boards dogs. At least she says she boards dogs. But we—my friend and I—think maybe she doesn't board them at all. We think she steals them in order to get a reward when she gives them back."

There was a brief pause at the other end of the line. "I see," the woman said. "Do you have any reason to suspect this?"

Willow told how Mrs. Clauson asked for more money for the poodle and she told what had happened with Jericho. "And now she has a Welsh Corgi," she said.

"Are your parents home? Do they know about this?"

"No," Willow said. "They're at the hospital with my sister."

The woman said she needed to think for a minute. She took Willow's name, address, and phone number and said she would call back soon.

She called in less than five minutes. "This is Andrea Wilson," she said. "A police officer is going to meet me at your house in ten minutes."

While they waited, Willow and Gretchen peered out the window.

"I hope Mrs. Clauson leaves the dog outside," Willow said.

"I've always wanted a dog or a cat," Gretchen said. "But Ryan has allergies so we can't have any animals." She sighed and spoke more softly. "A dog or a cat," she said wistfully.

"Something furry, a creature who would like me just the way I am, without wanting me to change."

"Who wants you to change?" Willow asked.

"Oh, you know how my folks are always after me to get better grades. I got a $B+$ on my science test yesterday and when my dad saw it, he said, 'What went wrong on this test? Why didn't you get an A?' Can you believe it? I thought a $B+$ was good, until he started in."

Willow knew what Gretchen was saying. Ever since kindergarten, Gretchen's parents had expected her to get all A's; anything less was not acceptable. And they nagged at her about her clothes and her hair.

She had often wondered why Gretchen's parents couldn't see what a super person Gretchen was. Why did they worry so about report cards? Gretchen wasn't in danger of flunking. She always got good grades so why would her parents want her to change?

"I like you just the way you are," Willow said.

"You do?" Gretchen said. She looked surprised.

In a flash of insight, Willow realized that she had been guilty of wishing Gretchen would change, too. She didn't care how many A grades Gretchen got and she thought Gretchen's hair was just fine but she had wanted Gretchen to have different religious views. She wanted Gretchen to think for herself more, instead of relying on her pastor to tell her what was right or wrong. She wished Gretchen would go to a less conservative church, one that didn't tell her exactly what to believe. Maybe, in her own way, she had been just as unfair to Gretchen as Gretchen's parents were.

"I've done a lot of thinking lately," Willow said slowly,

"about things I never thought about before. My ideas are changing and at first I wanted you to change, too. Now I see that it doesn't matter. We can be friends, even if we think differently about some things. What matters is how we feel about each other."

Gretchen looked relieved. "I was worried," she said. "You're the best friend I have and I thought I was going to lose you."

"No way."

"Believe it or not, I want you to keep on telling me the stuff you think about," Gretchen said. "Even reincarnation. And I won't tell anyone, if you ask me not to. I never did tell Pastor Farriday about your dreams."

"I've had some weird experiences," Willow said. "Not everyone will understand."

"Like what?"

Willow hesitated. She thought about the tunnel and the white light and the carnival. Should she tell Gretchen about those? Or about the voice she heard so clearly, when she was listening for Helen—the voice she couldn't identify?

"What's happened?" Gretchen said.

"Well, sometimes I feel a white light all around me."

"You mean, a halo? Like Jesus had?"

"I never thought of that," Willow said. "The pictures of Christ do show him with light around his head, don't they?"

Gretchen nodded. "All the saints have halos," she said.

"I'm no saint," Willow said, "but I do feel a light around me sometimes."

Gretchen looked impressed. "What else?" she said. "What else has happened?"

"I tried to send healing energy into Sarah. I held her hand and . . ."

"Faith healing?" Gretchen said. "I can't believe it! You tried faith healing with Sarah?"

"What do you mean by faith healing?"

"You know, the laying on of hands. Where you touch someone and Jesus works through your hands to heal that person. They do it in my church all the time."

"Does it work?"

"Sometimes. But I never dreamed you would believe in it."

"I didn't exactly do it that way."

"Isn't that what you said? You held her hand and the Lord worked through you to . . ."

"I sent the healing energy myself."

"Without," Gretchen said slowly, "any help from Jesus."

Willow nodded.

"What happened when you did it?"

"Sarah woke up and smiled at me. We talked. Of course, I can't prove that I helped her; she might have awakened then whether I was there or not."

"Faith healing without the faith," Gretchen said. "That's a new one."

"I had faith."

"But you just said you didn't expect any help from Jesus."

"Mrs. Evans believes in the healing power of love," Willow said. "That's what I was trying to use."

"Who's Mrs. Evans?"

Before Willow could explain, there was a knock on the

front door. Willow opened it and invited the police officer to come inside.

She told him everything that had happened with Mrs. Clauson and the dogs. By the time she finished, Andrea Wilson arrived.

They all went into the kitchen and looked out the window into Mrs. Clauson's backyard.

"That's her!" Andrea said. "That's Bonnie." She started for the door.

"Please don't go over there," the police officer said.

"I have to. I have to get Bonnie. She's probably scared to death, poor little thing. She's never been away from me before. I take her everywhere."

"We have no proof that Mrs. Clauson took Bonnie out of your car," the officer said. "I want you to wait for her to contact you; I want you to pay her the reward."

Andrea Wilson wrung her hands together. "I can't leave Bonnie there, now that I know where she is."

"If you take your dog now, it doesn't provide any evidence that Mrs. Clauson took her. It leaves her free to steal someone else's dog. The only way we can stop her is to catch her in the act of stealing a dog or to verify that she's the one who collected a reward in several cases."

Andrea Wilson hesitated. "I want to help," she said. "But I have to do what's fair to Bonnie, too. It might be days before that woman calls me. Bonnie's probably terrified."

"Maybe we can get Mrs. Clauson to call you right away," Willow said. "When she saw me look closely at Jericho, she called the owners and returned him that same day. Or at least I think that's what happened."

"If you show interest in this dog, too, Mrs. Clauson might be suspicious," the officer said. "I don't want to put you in any danger of retaliation before we have a clear case against her."

"Retaliation?" Willow said. How could Mrs. Clauson retaliate?

Then she remembered her conversation with Gretchen about what Mrs. Clauson might do with a dog if the owner didn't pay a reward. She looked at Muttsie. Would Mrs. Clauson try to sell Muttsie to a place that tests cosmetics on animals? Willow couldn't bear to think of such a possibility.

"I could be the one to talk to her," Gretchen said. "She doesn't know me. What if I knocked on her door and told her I'm looking for a lost Welsh Corgi? I could say I heard a dog bark in her yard and it sounded like mine."

Willow looked at Gretchen with admiration.

"It might work," the officer said.

After a brief discussion, Andrea Wilson went back home to be near her telephone. She called as soon as she arrived, to let them know she was there.

Willow and the officer waited while Gretchen went next door and spoke with Mrs. Clauson.

When Gretchen returned she said, "Mrs. Clauson says she's boarding the Welsh Corgi. She wouldn't let me look at it."

Five minutes later, Andrea called.

"I just had a call from a woman who says she found my dog. She tried to get me to raise the reward to $300 but when I said $200 is all I have, she agreed to take that. She wouldn't tell me her name. We're going to meet in half an hour."

The officer gave Andrea instructions, thanked Gretchen and Willow for their help, and left. Once more, the girls stood next to the window, watching the house next door.

Fifteen minutes later, they saw Mrs. Clauson leave the house and get in her car. She had the Welsh Corgi with her.

17

NUK UA em ennu en Xu ammu Xu.

The nonsense phrase repeated itself in her mind.

Nuk ua em ennu en Xu ammu Xu.

She looked again at what she had written. She didn't know how to pronounce it but somehow she knew the spelling was right. Had she been dreaming again? Maybe the words made sense as part of a dream.

She put the paper on her bedside table, lay back, and closed her eyes. Bit by bit, the dream came back to her.

Kalos hurried to get ready. She dipped her stick into the jar of kohl and carefully painted the green mixture around her eyes. She brushed her lips with red ochre and fastened her favorite beads around her neck.

Tiy entered, carrying two perfume cones. She attached

one of the cones to the top of Kalos's head and Kalos put the other one on Tiy's head.

Kalos picked up her lute and Tiy got her double pipe. They walked quickly into the central room.

The party had already begun. A harpist sang while she played her harp, and a group of dancers swayed and dipped. Kalos ate dates and grapes and nibbled on roasted rabbit.

When it was time for Kalos and Tiy to perform, Tiy looked nervous. Kalos smiled to reassure her as they carried their instruments to the center of the room and began to play. Tiy made one mistake, but no one except Kalos seemed to notice. The guests exclaimed how talented the two girls were and Kalos and Tiy, giddy with success and relief, fled back to their own quarters.

Kalos put down her lute, removed the perfume cone, and took off her wig. It felt wonderful to get the heavy, hot headdress off. She kept her own hair short, because of the heat, but for public occasions the plaited wig was necessary.

"Perhaps this will be the day of birth," Kalos said. "Wouldn't it be nice if our new sister or brother was born on such a happy day?"

Tiy nodded. "I will pray to Taweret," she said. "If the goddess of childbirth hears and agrees, the baby will be born."

Kalos did not try to dissuade her sister but she reserved her own prayers for Amun-Ra. Why direct her supplications to a lesser god, even a kindly one like Taweret, when she could go directly to the king of the gods?

The dream faded and Willow opened her eyes. That was all she could remember.

Quickly she jotted some notes. The wigs surprised her.

She thought wigs were a modern invention. Had Kalos worn a wig before, when she went to the temple?

She wondered about the new baby. If Tiy was Helen now, and Kalos was Willow now, was this new baby alive now, too? Was there, somewhere in the world today, another person who had once been her brother or sister? Maybe this child was the little girl she had glimpsed with Kalos and Tiy that night during the guided visualization in Mrs. Evans's office. What was her name? Huzein?

Willow wasn't sure she could handle another sibling. She'd been so excited when she met Helen; she felt the bond between them so strongly. Yet Helen didn't feel the same way at all. Although Helen was curious about Willow's ideas, she never tried to prove that they were sisters in another lifetime.

Willow was sorry she ever suggested the five o'clock experiment. She had hurt Gretchen's feelings badly over it that first night, and Helen never once tried to send Willow her thoughts. In her effort to contact someone from a past life, Willow nearly alienated her best friend in *this* life.

I won't make that mistake again, she decided. From now on, I'll care about the people who matter to me now. This life is the one that counts. The rest is only speculation.

She looked at the clock—4:30 A.M. She wondered if Sarah was awake. In three hours, Sarah would have the transplant. If the new marrow worked, it would completely replace the malignant bone marrow that had been producing cancerous white blood cells. Sarah could regain her health and live a normal life.

If the marrow didn't work . . . Willow refused to even

consider that possibility. The transplant had to work. It had to.

Willow's parents had written to the donor and thanked her. They sent the letter to the National Bone Marrow Program office in Minnesota, and asked that it be forwarded to the right person.

"Whatever happens with Sarah," they wrote, "we will always be grateful to you for giving her this chance."

According to Dr. Rogers, Sarah's odds of finding a non-relative donor with matching marrow were only one in 15,000. Yet it had happened. And, even though Sarah had lapsed into a coma for awhile, she got better and was now strong enough to have the transplant. So far, luck was with them.

Dr. Rogers had never said anything more to Willow about giving Sarah "false hopes for a cure." Willow wondered if Dr. Rogers thought it was a coincidence that Sarah came out of the coma after Willow talked to her. Would she have awakened at that time, regardless of what Willow said or did?

There was no way to prove that Willow's thoughts and love and healing energy had helped Sarah.

And there was no way to prove they didn't.

She decided to try it again. Right then. Maybe she could help Sarah be ready for the transplant. Willow thought of the white light and immediately, a glowing light encircled her. Although it was invisible, she felt its warmth and its power.

She thought of Sarah, lying in her hospital bed. She knew Sarah was in a special room that night, breathing sterile filtered air. In her mind, Willow imagined the room. "I give you the white light, Sarah," Willow whispered. "I send the light of love to heal you and keep you safe."

The light radiated from her and floated out the window, into the sky toward Sarah. In her mind, she saw the white light enter the hospital and creep under the plastic shields which hung like shower curtains around Sarah's bed.

Strangely, even though Willow sent the light to Sarah, this did not diminish the amount of light she felt around herself. She could give the healing love away without losing any of it.

She didn't understand how that could happen but she knew it was true. The white light was infinite; she could draw on it forever and there would still be more.

She breathed deeply. Having done what she could for Sarah, she felt relaxed and sleepy.

As Willow slipped over the edge from waking to sleeping, the dream returned.

Tired from the excitement of the party, Kalos slipped outside and walked quietly through the garden.

She thought of the new child who would soon join her family. She knew she would love this new baby, as she had always loved Tiy, and she hoped the baby would grow to love her, too. Even more, she hoped that perhaps this new child would understand her, as Tiy and her parents did not.

Tiy loved her, there was no doubt of that, but Tiy was often baffled when Kalos shared her thoughts and feelings.

Despite her friends and loving family, Kalos knew she was different from the others. She had inner strength; she had the ability to be happy regardless of circumstances.

When the others prayed, they asked favors or gave thanks. When Kalos prayed, she opened her heart and mind and felt Amun-Ra's light and energy flow into her.

Even at night, when all was dark and Amun-Ra traveled through the chambers of the underworld, Kalos could feel his light around her. It kept her safe; it gave her courage; it brought her joy.

Because of this, she knew she was special. She was glad that Amun-Ra had chosen her to receive his gift of light. She wondered if somewhere, perhaps in a land faraway, others shared her special gift. One day she hoped to speak to one of those others, to let that person know how she felt.

Kalos sat under a palm tree, leaned her head against the trunk, and closed her eyes. She wondered what she would say to another like herself, if she had the chance to speak.

High above her in the cloudless sky, Amun-Ra watched. Kalos looked up and smiled. She felt his power surround her, enter her, and reflect back to the sky.

Nuk ua em ennu en Xu ammu Xu.

That, she decided, is my message.

Nuk ua em ennu en Xu ammu Xu.

Willow stirred as the words came through once more. *Nuk ua em ennu en Xu ammu Xu.*

This time, she recognized the voice that spoke them. It was the voice of her dreams. It was herself in another lifetime. It was Kalos.

And then she knew.

Even in her half-waking, half-sleeping state, she realized it was not a nonsense phrase.

Nuk ua em ennu en Xu ammu Xu was a message from Kalos.

18

"HEY, QUEENIE."

Willow heard the words and knew Jeff was behind her. She decided to ignore him.

"What's the matter, Queenie? You too good to talk to your subjects?"

Willow walked faster. She was only two blocks from school. Once she got there, she thought Jeff would leave her alone.

He followed at her heels as she crossed the schoolyard. "Do you wear your royal jewels when you sleep?" he asked.

Willow turned to face him. "You aren't funny," she said. "All I did was ask a question about your speech; I don't see why you're making such a big deal out of it."

"Lo! The Queen speaketh!" Jeff said loudly. Several kids came to see what was happening. "Bow down!" Jeff said. "Bow down before the mighty Queen Willow." More kids gathered.

Willow clenched her teeth, determined not to be drawn into a scene with Jeff. I don't need this, she thought. Not today.

"What are your wishes, mighty Queen?" Jeff said.

The sun came out from behind a cloud and Jeff squinted as he looked at her.

Willow felt the sun on her back. Amun-Ra. Willow took a deep breath, turned and started to walk away.

Jeff's hand clamped down on her shoulder. "You can't leave," he said. His fingers dug into her shoulder. "We're going to crown you. Queen Willow. Queen of the . . ."

"Knock it off, Jeff!"

Willow spun around. Gretchen stood with her hands on her hips, her eyes flashing angrily. "You slime!" she said. "Don't you think Willow has enough problems?"

"Queens don't have problems."

"No? Cancer isn't a problem? Willow's sister is getting a bone marrow transplant today."

Jeff scowled. "I didn't know anything about any sister," he said.

"You act like you're still in kindergarten," Gretchen said. "Come on, Willow. Let's go to class."

The other kids dispersed as Willow and Gretchen walked away.

"Thanks," Willow said.

"My pleasure. I can't believe what a jerk Jeff is. And speaking of jerks, I got an answer to my letter."

"What letter?"

"The ad I answered. You know, the 16-year-old male."

"You actually sent him a letter?" Willow asked.

Gretchen nodded. "Fortunately, I had the sense not to use my real name. I decided once I found out who it is, I could always tell him my real name. Well, I found out, all right."

"Who is it?"

"You won't believe this."

"Who *is* it?"

"Pete."

"Pete Wellington?"

"The one and only."

Willow started to giggle.

"It isn't funny," Gretchen said, but she was laughing, too. "No more Personals ads for me," she said. "I'll have to find the love of my life some other way. Any news on Mrs. Clauson?"

"None. After you left last night, I watched her house until midnight, when my folks got home. She didn't leave again."

"I was hoping that officer would arrest her as soon as she took the reward money from Andrea Wilson."

"Me, too, but I suppose if Mrs. Clauson claims she found Bonnie, no one can prove otherwise."

"My pastor called this morning to ask if we wanted to keep Sarah's name on the prayer chain. I told him yes."

Willow smiled at Gretchen. It was comforting to know that all over the city today, people would be thinking of Sarah, praying for her, sending good thoughts to her.

"I wasn't sure if you'd be at school today," Gretchen said.

"It doesn't do any good for me to sit at the hospital. The time will go faster for me if I'm thinking of something else."

"You may have plenty to think about," Gretchen said. "I

heard that this is going to be Mr. Barclay's Hell Week."

Willow moaned. Not that, too, on top of everything else. Once each year, Mr. Barclay, their history teacher, assigned a major project to each student and gave them only one week to do the work.

Each year, older students warned the seventh graders about the project, referring to it in menacing tones as, "Barclay's Hell Week." They declared that the only way to get a passing grade on a Hell Week project was to work so hard you nearly died from the effort.

Each year, the projects were different so that students whose older brothers and sisters had previously survived Hell Week weren't able to help. Each year, according to the older kids, the projects were harder.

Willow and Gretchen found their seats in history class and waited.

"Good morning, class," Mr. Barclay said. "I understand there's a rumor going around that this is the day you get your special project assignment, sometimes referred to as Hell Week."

Willow looked at Gretchen.

"I prefer to think of these assignments as heavenly opportunities for learning," Mr. Barclay said.

Everyone groaned.

"Here it comes," Gretchen whispered.

"This year," Mr. Barclay said, "our projects will be written reports. Each will be different."

He went on to explain that they had three choices:

1. Write a paper on one country's history of agriculture.
2. Write a paper on one country's history of religion.

3. Write a paper on the history of literature, art, and music
    in one country.

"The papers must be a minimum of ten pages long," Mr.
Barclay said, "with a bibliography of at least five sources. And
the country cannot be the United States."

The students grumbled some more. Hell Week was even
worse than they expected.

"Here is a list of the acceptable countries," Mr. Barclay
said. "Each country appears three times, followed by the word
agriculture, religion, or art. As soon as you select the country
and topic you want to study, write your name beside it and
cross it off the list. Only one person will be allowed to do a
paper on each topic."

He gave the list to a boy in the front row, who looked at
it, shrugged helplessly, and passed it on without choosing his
topic. By the time the list got to Willow, only three topics had
been crossed off.

Quickly she read the list of available countries: Argentina,
Brazil, Czechoslovakia, Denmark, Egypt . . . As soon as she
got to Egypt, she knew what she would do. She crossed, *Egypt*,
religion off the list, wrote her name, and passed the list to
Gretchen.

In her notebook, she wrote, "Hell Week Project: The history of religion in Egypt." All around her, kids muttered about
the unfairness of Barclay's Hell Week.

Even Gretchen, who usually didn't complain about
school, frowned at the list as she tried to decide. "I can't believe
this," she said. "I'll never finish in only one week."

Willow didn't answer. She would never have admitted it
when everyone else was so upset, but secretly, she could hardly

wait to start. She wanted to learn the history of religion in Egypt. She wanted to know if there was a god called Amun-Ra. And she wanted to be involved in a big project, even a hard one, to keep her mind occupied. If she was reading about the past religions of Egypt, she wouldn't be able to worry about Sarah.

19

"THE TRANSPLANT went smoothly," Dr. Rogers said, "with no complications."

Willow wanted to shout but shouting was frowned on in a hospital so she hugged her mother instead. Then she hugged her father. And then, in an outburst of glad relief, she hugged Dr. Rogers.

"May I see her?" Willow asked.

"We want you to see her," Dr. Rogers said. "You'll need to scrub down and wear a mask and gown, or stay outside the sterile room and talk to her through the plastic."

"I'll scrub down."

"You understand, of course, that today's transplant was only the first step," Dr. Rogers said. "It will be several weeks before we can say with any certainty that the transplant is a success. There's always the possibility of infection or liver failure and more than half the patients develop some degree of GVHD."

GVHD, Willow knew, meant Graft-Versus-Host Disease. The dangers of GVHD had been explained to them many times. Why couldn't Dr. Rogers just let them be glad for this one success, instead of reminding them of all the potential problems?

"She made it this far," Mr. Paige said. "We're thankful for that."

For the next three days, Willow used every free minute to work on her Hell Week project. When she visited Sarah, she talked through the plastic, rather than scrubbing down and donning the mask and gloves. It was faster and she needed every possible minute. Sarah understood. She had been through Mr. Barclay's Hell Week herself, two years earlier.

Willow spent her time at the public library, or at home reading the library books. She had stacks of 3×5 cards with notes about the religion of early Egypt.

Gretchen called nightly to complain that Mr. Barclay was a slave driver. Willow just listened. Ever since she began her Hell Week project, she'd been fascinated by what she learned.

That first day, in one of the library books, she read, "In the New Kingdom, Amun-Ra became the supreme state god, the King of the Gods."

Willow's breath caught. There he was in print: Amun-Ra. King of the Gods, just as Kalos had said.

Quickly, she turned to the chart of dates at the front of the book. The New Kingdom went from 1567 to 1085 BC.

The New Kingdom *ended* more than 3,000 years ago. Was it possible that she could accurately recall details of a lifetime from over 3,000 years ago?

Where had her soul been in the meantime, during all the years between Kalos and Willow? Had she been a man with a dagger, riding a white horse? A woman in a green gown, admiring paintings and sculptures? She reminded herself that just because there once was a god named Amun-Ra, it didn't prove that Willow had lived in ancient Egypt.

She continued to read. And then, on the third day, she found it. Willow felt a chill go up the back of her neck as she read the words. "One of the great architectural wonders of the world was the Temple at Karnak which was designed so that, on the day of the winter solstice, the rising sun shone directly on the temple's altar."

There was a picture of the Temple at Karnak. She recognized it immediately. As Willow looked at the picture she felt just like she did when she looked at a photograph of her old house, where the Paiges lived before Sarah got sick and they had to move closer to the hospital.

Karnak. She looked at the map of Egypt. Karnak was on the east side of the Nile River, right in the middle of Egypt. Last year she would have called it a foreign country. Now she thought of it as her other home.

She didn't read only about religion. She also looked for details of the daily life of the people who lived then. She found descriptions of the kind of house Kalos had lived in: made of mudbrick, with three sections. The outer room was for greeting strangers; the central room was for entertaining friends and the ast room was the family's private quarters. Willow remembered how Kalos and Tiy got ready in their private room and then went to the middle room to play their instruments for their guests. Detail after detail in the books were just as she had remembered them in her dreams.

In her report, Willow summarized the earlier religious beliefs and gave an in-depth report on Amun-Ra. She ended with a two-page description which, she said, might have been written by herself, if she had lived during that time.

"My name is Kalos," she began, "and my favorite god is Amun-Ra. Each year, on the day of the winter solstice, I go with my family to the Temple at Karnak."

The words flowed easily as she described what she wore and the offerings she carried. Most of all, she told about her feelings. It was easy to pretend she was Kalos as she wrote; she had only to remember her dreams.

The Hell Week projects were due on Friday. On Thursday night, as Willow was copying hers over in ink, she heard loud voices outside. Looking out, she saw a police car in front of Mrs. Clauson's house. The same officer who had come to meet Andrea Wilson stood on Mrs. Clauson's porch. So did a fat woman with red hair.

"That's her," the woman cried. "I'd know her anywhere." The woman started to open Mrs. Clauson's door but the officer restrained her. "Where's Jojo?" the woman cried. "What have you done with Jojo?"

"I don't know what you're talking about," Mrs. Clauson said. The door was open less than six inches and she stood so that the woman couldn't see in.

"She took my dog!" the woman insisted. "I saw her. Jojo was in my car and I stopped at the grocery store to get a loaf of bread. I didn't lock the car because I knew I'd only be gone a few minutes. When I came out of the store, I saw this woman drive away with Jojo. I called to her but she didn't stop."

"You are mistaken," Mrs. Clauson said.

"I got your license number," the woman said.

"Then you deny that you have this woman's dog?" the officer said.

"Of course I deny it. I don't know anything about her dog. And if you don't quit harassing me, I'll call the Chief of Police and complain."

A dog barked.

"That's him," the red-haired woman said. "Jojo's in there; I hear him."

"You hear my dog," Mrs. Clauson said.

Willow knew that wasn't true. Mrs. Clauson didn't have a dog.

"We can't go in without a search warrant," the officer said.

Willow left the window and looked quickly around the room. A bouquet of flowers for Sarah sat on the coffee table. One of Sarah's friends had brought it that afternoon and asked Willow to see that Sarah got it. Willow grabbed the vase of flowers and ran out the front door. Sarah wouldn't mind, not if the flowers did what Willow hoped they would do.

As she hurried toward Mrs. Clauson's yard, the red-haired woman began to shout. "Let me in!" she demanded.

The dog barked again.

Willow walked quickly up the porch steps. "Hello, Officer," she said, and he nodded.

"Excuse me," she said to the red-haired woman. "I have a delivery for Mrs. Clauson." The woman stepped aside.

"Not now," Mrs. Clauson said.

"These came for you," Willow said, "and I promised I'd bring them over as soon as you got home."

"Come back later. I—I'm in my bathrobe."

"That's OK. Here, I'll just hand them to you quickly." Willow lifted the vase and held it toward the door.

Mrs. Clauson opened her door far enough to put out an arm. She reached for the flowers.

The moment Mrs. Clauson's hand touched the vase, Willow yelled, "Here, Jojo."

Instantly, the red-haired woman called, too. "Jojo! Come!"

Mrs. Clauson tried to close the door but she moved too slowly. Before she could stop him, a yellow terrier bolted between her legs and flung himself at the woman.

"Jojo," the woman said and promptly burst into tears.

The dog gave excited little yips.

The woman picked him up and hugged him. "I told you she had him," she said to the officer. "I know the sound of my own dog's voice."

The officer reached over and looked at the tag that hung from the terrier's collar. Willow looked, too. It said, "JOJO", followed by a woman's name and telephone number.

The officer turned to Mrs. Clauson, who stood in the doorway, watching. "I'd like you to come down to the station with me," he said.

Mrs. Clauson's shoulders sagged. She seemed to shrink right before Willow's eyes. "I can't get by on my Social Security," she said. "People who feed a dog can afford to help me. I only take pampered pets, from fancy cars or big houses.

I never . . ." She was still talking as the officer helped her into the back seat of the patrol car.

He turned back to the red-haired woman. "Do you want to press charges?" he asked.

The woman hesitated, then nodded. "Yes," she said. "I want to be sure she doesn't do this to someone else."

Willow watched them drive away. Then she picked up the phone and called Gretchen.

ON FRIDAY, a few kids had excuses why their Hell Week projects weren't finished but most of the class turned their papers in. Willow's was longer than the ten required pages. Even so, she was nervous about what Mr. Barclay would think of it. It was not, she knew, a usual report. She had written far more than the information she'd found in the library books.

Her history class was first period. At lunch time, as she was leaving the cafeteria, Mr. Barclay saw her.

"I read your report this morning," he said. "It's one of the best I've ever seen. Some of your descriptions are so vivid, they sound as if you really lived in Egypt during the time of the New Kingdom."

I did, Willow thought. But she couldn't tell Mr. Barclay that.

20

"SARAH IS dead." Dr. Rogers spoke slowly, forcing the words past his lips. "Liver failure."

It was one week after the transplant.

This can't be true, Willow thought. It's a terrible mistake. But as she looked at the tears trickling down her father's cheeks and at the incredible pain in her mother's eyes, she knew there was no mistake.

"I thought she was going to make it," Dr. Rogers said. "I'm—sorry." His voice broke. Through her tears, Willow saw that he was weeping, too.

That night, Willow went into Sarah's room. She touched Sarah's pillow; she ran her hand across the top of Sarah's dresser. When no more tears came, she sat alone, staring out the window.

A full moon glowed like a ceiling lamp, dimly lighting

the shrubs and grass. The same way it lit the road for Kalos when she went to the temple, Willow thought.

Would Sarah have another life some time? Would she live again in a different body? Would she stand in a faraway place, in a distant time, and look up at the moon?

Willow thought a belief in reincarnation ought to make it easier to say good-bye to her sister, but it didn't help at all. No matter how many other lives Sarah might live, she would never again have *this* life. She would never again be Sarah Peony, sister of Willow Sweet Pea. She would never live in this house or sleep in this bed. She would not grow up and wear a cap and gown at graduation. If Willow got married some day, Sarah would not be there to be the Maid of Honor.

Maybe Dr. Rogers was right. Maybe the white light had no healing powers. It had not helped Sarah. Neither had Gretchen's prayer chain.

Still, she was glad she'd told Sarah about the white light, and how she could feel it around her any time she wanted to. She was glad she told her about Kalos, too, and about seeing Grandma and Grandpa.

At least, Willow thought, I don't have to beat myself up for not saying things to her when I had the chance. There wasn't much I could do to help her, but I did what I could. And it helped a little. It gave her hope. Perhaps it gave her peace.

THE PAIGES held a memorial service for Sarah the next Saturday at Pinecone Park. A tape recorder played Sarah's favorite songs and two of Sarah's friends read brief poems.

Willow held a cluster of white helium balloons. At the end of the service, she released them. The music played while the balloons rose into the cloudless blue sky.

Willow stared until the last balloon climbed out of sight.

Behind her, someone said, "I'm sorry about your sister." It was Mrs. Evans.

"I've thought of you often," Mrs. Evans went on.

"You have?"

"Yes. I try to meditate every day and as part of my meditation, I always send my thoughts to friends who are in difficult situations."

"How?" Willow asked. "How do you send your thoughts?"

"I get in a comfortable chair, where I know I won't be disturbed, and I close my eyes. Then I visualize the person I want to help and I send my thoughts to that person."

Willow swallowed. "What time did you send me your thoughts?" she asked.

"I try to meditate as soon as I get to my office, usually around 8:30 every morning."

"Oh." At 8:30 in the morning, Willow was in school.

"Of course, I don't always have time then. One day, a week or two ago, I had such a full schedule that I didn't meditate until just before I went home. Five o'clock."

"What thought did you send to me? Exactly?"

"I always say the same thing: *I am thinking of you. I think of you every day and wish the best for you and your sister.*"

Willow felt goosebumps on the back of her neck. So she *had* received a message. She did pick up those words, via mental telepathy, when she was trying to contact Helen. She had believed the words were from Helen when all along it was Mrs. Evans who was thinking of her.

"I heard you," Willow said. "I knew someone was sending that message to me."

"I'm sorry that the good thoughts were not enough to keep Sarah here with you longer."

"I tried to give the white light to Sarah," Willow said. "I felt it around me so strongly and I could see it surrounding her, too, but it didn't do any good. It didn't help her."

"You don't know that. Perhaps it made Sarah feel safe and unafraid. Maybe when her liver failed, she was able to follow the light out of this life and into the next."

"I hope you're right."

Since other people were waiting to talk to Willow, Mrs. Evans started to move on.

"Wait," Willow said, putting her hand on Mrs. Evans's arm.

Mrs. Evans paused.

"I had another dream about Kalos," Willow said. "And I think . . ."

"Yes?"

"I think she sent me a message. Does that ever happen?"

"Often. When I do regressions, I have my patients ask the people they visualize whether there is any message for them."

"This wasn't a regression. It was a dream. A plain old dream."

"Dreams are important. Sometimes our dreams can help us make decisions about what we should do."

Willow thought about that for a moment. Her dreams

didn't show her what to do. Mostly, they just confused her.

"Do you want to tell me about the message from Kalos?" Mrs. Evans asked.

"I can't remember it exactly. It's in a different language. Egyptian, I think. I wrote it down; it's in my notebook at home. It has some weird spellings, like x-u."

"If you want to send it to me, I'll do some research and see if I can translate it for you."

"Thanks," Willow said. "I'll send it tomorrow."

Willow turned to see who else was waiting to talk to her. It was a group of kids from Sarah's class. One of them was Pete Wellington.

Willow clenched her teeth angrily. A fat lot of good it did for Pete to show up now. If he was going to come at all, why didn't he do it when it might have helped Sarah? She was tempted to say that, except she didn't want to start an argument here, knowing how it would distress her mother.

"I'm really sorry," Pete mumbled, as he looked at Willow's feet.

"Thank you for coming," Willow said.

Pete's head jerked up and his eyes met hers. "I'm sorry," he said again. "I—I wish I'd gone to see her, before."

To her surprise, Willow felt sorry for him. It would be terrible to know you had failed to help a friend who needed you, and to carry that regret all your life.

THE NEXT day her parents said they wanted to get away for a time and the three of them left, just like that, without reservations or anything, and went to the ocean for a week. They said Willow could make up her schoolwork when they got back.

Willow walked for miles up the beach, exploring tidepools and throwing a stick for Muttsie to retrieve. She ate clam chowder and watched some fishermen and helped her dad put out a crab pot.

In the evenings, they built a fire in the fireplace of the rented cabin and played three-handed Hearts. They read books or made popcorn or sat by the fire and told stories.

One night they talked about Sarah.

"We were lucky to have Sarah," Mrs. Paige said. "I didn't want to let her go yet but I'm glad we had her, even for such a short time."

"We still have our memories," Mr. Paige said. "Remember the time Grandma and Grandpa said they would take all of us out for dinner to celebrate Sarah's birthday? And Sarah got to choose where we would go."

Willow smiled in the firelight. It was a favorite family story and even though she'd heard it dozens of times, she always liked to hear it again.

"It was her sixth birthday," Mrs. Paige said. "I was glad that I didn't have to cook a fancy dinner. I suggested all the best restaurants, and Sarah said she needed to think about it."

"I hoped she would choose Wendy's or Pizza Hut," Willow said.

"Not me," Mrs. Paige said. "I hoped she would pick a good seafood restaurant, with a view."

"She kept us all in suspense until the day before her birthday," Mr. Paige said. "Then Grandma told Sarah she had to make up her mind or it would be too late to get a reservation.

And that's when Sarah said . . ." Here Mr. Paige paused and then all three of them said Sarah's line together:

"What I really want is to stay home on my birthday and eat canned spaghetti."

"Canned spaghetti!" Mrs. Paige said. "When we could have gone to the fanciest restaurant in town."

They laughed together, the three of them, as shadows from the firelight played tag across their faces. It felt good to laugh again. It had been such a long time since Willow and her parents had laughed together. She wished Sarah were there to laugh with them.

As if she were thinking the same thing, Mrs. Paige said, "When we remember the good times, I feel as if Sarah is still with us."

"We can visit her any time we want," Mr. Paige said, "through our memories."

Just like my carnival, Willow thought. I can go there whenever I want, too.

And the white light? Could she still feel it?

She hadn't felt the light since the night before Sarah's transplant, when she visualized sending it to Sarah in the hospital. In her shock and grief since Sarah's death, she had not cared about white lights or mental telepathy or past lives.

Now she wondered if the light was still there. Since it failed to save Sarah's life, was it powerless, after all?

The moment she tried to feel it again, it was there. Once more, she glowed with an inner radiance. Once more, she felt glad, and strong. The white light couldn't save Sarah's life but it could give her the strength to endure Sarah's death. She would face whatever life might bring, and still feel joy.

Like the carnival, the light came from within her and nothing external could ever take it away. For the rest of her life, it would give her courage and bring her joy.

That night, she dreamed of Sarah, but in the dream, Sarah's name wasn't Sarah. It was Huzein.

Huzein and Kalos stood together early one morning, watching the sun rise. Kalos, who was older than in the previous dreams, smiled fondly at her younger sister. Huzein was so much like herself. She was everything Kalos had hoped she would be, before she was born.

"I will tell you a secret," Huzein said. "Of all our family, you are most dear to me."

"And you to me," Kalos said.

Willow didn't have to write the dream down in order to remember it. She knew she would never forget.

Huzein and Sarah were the same. One soul in two bodies. She had found Sarah in more than one lifetime; she would find her again.

21

ON THEIR way home from the beach, the Paiges stopped at a nursery and bought fifteen peony plants, one for each year of Sarah's life. They dug a new flower bed in their front yard, added mulch and fertilizer, and planted the peonies.

"It's a fitting memorial," Mr. Paige said, as he tamped the dirt down with his shoes.

"The Sarah Peony Paige Memorial Garden," Willow said, as she covered the area with mulch.

Mrs. Paige wiped tears from her cheeks.

There were two letters waiting for Willow. The first was from Scotland. It said:

Dear Willow,

    Last week I had the flu. My temperature was 103°. One night, when I was so sick, I had the strangest dream. I had long black hair, in tight ringlets, and a white linen dress. I sat at a loom, weaving, in a strange house made of clay. I didn't look at all like me, yet I knew it was me.

I can't be sure but I think maybe I dreamed of Tiy. Please write again soon and tell me what you've learned about Egypt.

Love,
Helen (Your Egyptian sister)

The second letter was from Mrs. Evans.

Dear Willow:

I found the phrase you sent me, from your dream.

"Nuk uā em ennu en Xu ammu Xu" is from The Egyptian Book of the Dead. *It means, "I am one of those shining beings who lives in light."*

I hope this helps you.

Mrs. Evans

Willow read the translation again and then sat quietly, with the letter in her lap. "I am one of those shining beings who lives in light."

So Kalos had felt the white light, too. She felt it and she knew it made her special. She wanted Willow to know, to recognize her own specialness.

A shining being.

I do know, Willow thought. I know that life is like the carnival, full of music and laughter and joy. All I have to do is open the door and experience it.

I knew it then, in ancient Egypt, and I know it now.

I am one of those shining beings who lives in light.

ABOUT THE AUTHOR

PEG KEHRET lives in an old farmhouse in Washington State with her husband, Carl, and a variety of pets. While she writes, her husband restores antique player pianos and nickelodeons. She is the author of various magazine articles, adult books, and plays, in addition to her popular books for young readers. Her Minstrel titles include *Nightmare Mountain* and *Sisters, Long Ago*. Her award-winning plays have been produced in all fifty states and Canada.